MUZZLED

ALSO by DAVID ROSENFELT

MUZZLED

David Rosenfelt

MINOTAUR BOOKS
NEW YORK

First published in the United States by Minotaur Books, an imprint of St. Martin's Publishing Group

MUZZLED. Copyright © 2020 by Tara Productions, Inc. All rights reserved. Printed in the United States of America. For information, address St. Martin's Publishing Group, 120 Broadway, New York, NY 10271.

ISBN 9781250257116

MUZZLED

The boat was in international waters, just outside the three-mile limit.

The nearest land was Long Beach Island in New Jersey, where it had sailed from. The fifty-foot luxury boat had the name *Doral* emblazoned on it.

Some might call the *Doral* a yacht. One of the people who would call it that was its owner, Alex Vogel, because *yacht* sounded better than *boat*. Vogel's deceased parents had been named Doris and Alex, hence the name of the craft. They had struggled financially most of their lives, and Alex junior wished that they had lived to see how successful he had become.

He especially wished they had lived to see and board the *Doral*. His mother would have been embarrassed to have a boat named after her and Alex's father, but she would secretly have loved it and bragged about it to her bridge club.

The day was sunny and calm, and the *Doral* was simply floating languidly on the water. It was a motorboat, but the motor was off and had been for a while.

There would be no obvious reason for any other passing craft to think anything was wrong. No SOS signal had been sent, and the boat was not behaving erratically. It was actually not "behaving" at all; it was just drifting in the relatively placid water.

A passing boat, smaller at thirty-five feet and carrying four people, got within a hundred yards or so. They waved, since people on boats generally like to appear friendly, but no one was on deck to wave back. That didn't seem odd to the wavers; perhaps the people on the other boat were belowdecks, having lunch or doing whatever.

Then one of them noticed what appeared to be a figure of a man lying on the deck. It seemed like an unusual position for the person to be in. So they got a pair of binoculars and saw to their horror that the man might have been unconscious and had a large stain on his shirt that looked like blood. He might have been worse than unconscious.

They had no way of knowing that two men were actually on the *Doral,* on the other side of the deck and out of their line of sight. Each of the men had a bullet hole in his chest and had been dead for almost thirty minutes. Their waving days were over.

The people on the boat were understandably worried, and they moved closer to confirm what they believed before sending out an SOS.

They were about a hundred and fifty feet from the *Doral* when it exploded.

The bodies of the three passengers said to be on the *Doral,* all pharmaceutical executives, were nowhere to be found and would likely never be recovered, since the depth of the water at the place of the incident was almost five thousand feet. Identifications were not necessary, since a number of witnesses saw the three men as they left the dock.

The Coast Guard conducted a brief investigation, then punted to the New Jersey State Police. Much to everyone's surprise, they quickly declared it to be a likely multiple homicide. Elements in the recovered wreckage were clearly connected to a man-made explosive device. A bomb, and not a mechanical failure, they concluded, had blown the boat out of the water.

The word *likely* was added because it was impossible to know if the device was intentionally detonated. Possibly whoever was responsible had not intended to set it off, and the explosion was accidental.

But if that was the case, why take a bomb out on a pleasure craft off the coast of New Jersey?

It did not take them long to learn the answer, though they did not reveal it publicly.

Secrecy was paramount while they conducted their search.

Dad, can we go bungee jumping?" Ricky asked.

I've got to be careful with my answer. He's asking a serious question, albeit one that horrifies me. I can't overreact, hurt his feelings, embarrass him, or appear dismissive. I need to imagine how my response will sound when he repeats it to a therapist later in life.

"Are you nuts?" is what I finally come out with. It's possible that I didn't fulfill my previously stated criteria for a good answer. So I add, "Bungee jumping?"—a question that merely repeats the subject but otherwise does nothing to advance the conversation or get me off the parental hook. It seems like I spend half my life hanging on parental hooks.

He nods, undeterred. "Will and I watched some people doing it on television. I think it was in Mexico, or Europe, or somewhere. There was this big cliff, and they just jumped. It was really cool. Will said we should try it."

Will Rubenstein is Ricky's best friend and clearly a negative influence on him. I, Andy Carpenter, need to intervene and establish control over my son.

"You should speak to your mother about this," I say. Laurie Collins is my wife and Ricky's mother; she's probably more capable of establishing the control that I mentioned.

"She said I should talk to you. And she laughed when she said it."

I'm not surprised that she laughed. Laurie knows my feelings about scary things; she recognizes that I am scared of them. I'm for some reason supposed to be embarrassed by that. But the truth is that I don't know why everyone isn't scared of them . . . they're scary. The entire concept of what people refer to as "adventure" or "living on the edge" is one that I don't understand.

People do things like bungee jumping or skydiving or surfing thirty-foot waves because those things are dangerous. The excitement lies in the fear, the risk . . . without it those things would not exist. For example, there is another way to reach the ground from a plane rather than jumping out of it: you could just land.

The truth is that fear of all of these "adventures" is legitimate; if things don't go well, the practitioner, the adventurer, could die.

And what if they do go well? The bungee cord holds and isn't a few feet too long. Or the parachute opens. Or the waves don't swallow the surfer up and turn him into shark food. What then? The person lives? Yes, because that's the goal . . . survival is the goal.

There are other ways to continue to live. For example, bowling. Or Ping-Pong. Or watching television. Or eating pistachio nuts. There are a lot more, but I've just listed four of the best, except for bowling.

I had a roommate in my freshman year of college whose goal was to climb the highest mountain on every continent. My goal at the time was to change roommates. He would frequently tell me that taking risks for adventure, pushing the envelope, was what life was all about. Anything else, he would say, was "just existing."

I'm not sure when "existing" got such a bad name. What's the alternative? It's the only thing I can think of that is both necessary for life and carries a negative connotation. No one says that breathing is a waste of time, or eating is for suckers.

Bottom line is that no matter what you say about someone, if the speech ends with "but he no longer exists," that's simply not a positive.

A story was on the news this morning about six guys who went from South America to Antarctica across Drake Passage in a rowboat. I never even knew that Drake had a passage; I did know he had cake.

The six men handled forty-foot waves and giant whales, all of which could have tipped their canoe over at any time. If they had gone into the frigid water, the estimate is that they would have died in two to five minutes.

These half dozen lunatics wanted to be the first people to ever make this trip. By definition, I never want to be the first at anything. That's because there is invariably a reason no one has ever done it before. You never hear that a person is the first to attend a great concert or read a great book or watch a football game. That's because if something is good, everybody wants to do it.

But back to the matter at hand. I need to talk Ricky out of the bungee-jumping idea without sounding like a dictator or, worse, a wimp. The best way to do that is to shift the blame.

"Let's see what Will's dad thinks of the idea," I say. Will's father, Brian, is a friend of mine. As a pediatrician he has taken an oath to do no harm; there is obviously no way he will approve of the bungee-jumping idea.

"So if Will can do it, so can I?"

"If Will can do it, we'll sit down with your mother and have a family discussion." No sense shifting the blame to one person when I can shift it to two.

He nods, apparently satisfied, and switches topics. "You want to throw the football around?"

I nod. "It's risky, but I'll try it."

Ricky gets the football and we go out into the driveway. He throws a perfect spiral, with some zip on the ball. I'm not an expert on the expected football-talent level of eleven-year-olds, but I think he's pretty darn good.

I dread the day he will want to play high school football and I try to talk Laurie into letting him. She'll think it's too dangerous, that concussions are too prevalent. I'll tell her that he should play because just sitting back and watching others is simply existing.

We've been doing it for about twenty minutes, and my arm feels like it's about to fall off. Mercifully, Laurie calls out from the house, "Andy, Beth Morris on the phone."

"Can you tell her I'll call her back after I have shoulder-reattachment surgery?"

"I tried that, but she says it's important, that it can't wait."

We stop throwing and I go in the house. As I pass Laurie I say, "We're doing a family bungee jump next week."

Beth Morris is involved in dog rescue, as am I. I run a rescue organization called the Tara Foundation, named after my own incredibly wonderful golden retriever. Beth is in a different area; her mission in life is to reunite lost dogs with their owners.

"Hi, Beth," I say when I pick up the phone. Sometimes my conversational talents stun even myself.

"Andy, I have a problem, a major problem. I need to talk to you."

"Is it about a dog?"

"In a way it is."

"Which one?"

"Andy, I'm not calling you because you rescue dogs. I'm calling you because you're a criminal attorney."

"Oh."

I don't know Beth Morris very well.

I've probably talked to her about fifty times, fifty of which have involved dogs. I don't know where she lives, whether she's married or has kids, or whether she roots for the Giants or Jets or none of the above.

I do know that she is incredibly dedicated to what for her has become an all-consuming hobby. She told me that she once found a stray dog and successfully located the distraught owner. Making that connection and returning the dog was incredibly rewarding for her, so she started doing it regularly.

Beth has established an amazing network of dog people, rescue groups, social media contacts, and so on to facilitate the process. Her success rate is remarkable, especially considering that quite a few owners have just abandoned their dogs and do not want to be reunited with them.

Since my partner, Willie Miller, and I started the Tara Foundation, we obviously wind up with stray dogs all the time. We want to place these dogs in new, forever homes, but there is always the chance that a distraught owner is out there looking for one of the dogs.

Often those owners would have no idea that their pets are with us, and that is where Beth comes in. She has taken it upon herself to find out who the original owners are and determine whether they are anxiously looking for their canine family member.

Often, they are not. Sometimes they are.

I didn't know that Beth was aware that I am a criminal defense attorney. I don't think I've ever mentioned it to her.

I've been trying to retire from that for a while now; I possess a unique combination of laziness and wealth that enables me to do so. Unfortunately, I keep getting dragged into cases for a variety of reasons.

Many of the cases I have taken have become prominent in the media, so maybe that's how Beth knows about me. I don't know if she wants to hire me or just ask for advice. I'm hoping for the latter, but she sounded nervous, so I'm worried that more is involved than a simple consultation.

Beth is at the house within twenty minutes; she tells me she lives in Fair Lawn, just across the river from our house in Paterson. I wanted to meet here so that Laurie could also hear what is going on. Laurie is a former cop and my main investigator when I take on a case. If this is a police matter, she'll likely have more to offer than I will.

Laurie has never met Beth, so I introduce them. After that, we wait a few minutes while Beth pets Tara and Sebastian, our basset hound. If we have to wait until Tara and Sebastian get tired of being petted, we're talking months.

Once we're settled in the kitchen with coffee, Beth gets to it. "Are you familiar with Lucy?"

I shake my head. "I don't think so; what's her last name?"

She smiles. "She doesn't have one. She's a yellow lab. You have her at the Foundation."

"Oh. I think I know which one she is." I'm not nearly as

involved with the day-to-day workings of the foundation as Willie Miller and his wife, Sondra, are. I'm pretty much in a constant guilt about it, but they don't seem to mind.

"Willie asked if I could help find her owner," Beth says. "That was about two weeks ago. I've been working it ever since. Tough case."

I'm sort of relieved in that this seems to be about a dog after all, but Beth had said it was more than that, so all I can do is wait until she fully explains it.

"There's a chip in the dog, but it traces to a veterinarian who retired and sold his practice. He has since died, so the process became more difficult, but I finally tracked it down to an owner named Richard Myers. I couldn't reach Myers, but I did find his ex-wife, who knew about Lucy, but who said that when they split up, they gave her away. That was three years ago."

It feels like three years since Beth started telling this story, but all I can do is wait.

"Do you know who they gave Lucy to?" Laurie asks.

Beth nods. "Alex Vogel."

She looks at Laurie and me as if expecting a reaction, as if we're supposed to recognize the name. I don't, but Laurie says, "The name sounds familiar, but I can't place it."

"You remember that boating accident a few weeks ago in the ocean off Long Beach Island?"

I remember it well, as does Laurie. The media coverage was substantial, even hitting national outlets. "It was considered a multiple homicide," Laurie says.

Beth nods. "Right. I only sort of heard about it at the time, but I've since googled it. Alex Vogel was one of the three men on the boat."

"Does he have any family members who might want Lucy?"

"I don't know," she says. "But we'll be able to find out."

"How?"

"Alex Vogel called me; he wants his dog."

It's now clear why Beth wanted to talk to me.

Receiving a phone call from a murder victim can be disconcerting. Of course, there is little likelihood that it actually happened in this case, but one never knows.

"Tell us more," I say, which constitutes an unnecessary prompt.

"I got a phone call from a man who identified himself as Daniel Simmons. He said that he saw the story about Lucy online, and he was sure that it was his dog."

"How could he be sure?" Laurie asks.

"He said he was positive, so I asked him a few questions. For one thing, he told me her real name was Aggie. I know that was true from the chip, and from the original owner. And when I called her Aggie, she clearly responded to the name."

"That's all?" I ask.

Beth shakes her head. "No. He also knew that she has a plate in her leg from a surgery. Her leg had been badly broken, and that was the only way it could be stabilized. I know that from the vet records."

"Maybe it was someone else who currently owns the dog. Vogel could have given her away himself, to this Daniel Simmons, after he got it from those other people."

Beth shakes her head again. "There's something else. When

I researched Vogel, there was a video of him online, giving a speech at some pharmaceutical convention. Something technical about testing protocols. He was a . . ."

"And?"

"The phone voice and the voice in the video were the same; I'm positive. He has a faint Boston accent, and the pitch is identical."

"You can tell that from one phone call?" Laurie asks, sharing my skepticism.

Beth nods. "I listened to him very carefully. You'd have no way of knowing this, but I have a master's in speech therapy. It's my field of expertise."

"What did you tell him?" I ask.

"Well, he is in Pennsylvania, or at least that's what he said. He asked if I could find someone to transport the dog to him. He said he'd pay all expenses, and all costs I've incurred to date. I said I couldn't possibly do that; he'd have to come meet me and Lucy, or Aggie, personally. That seemed like the best thing to do until I talked to you."

There are a number of possibilities here, and most are not particularly worrisome. For one thing, despite what Beth sees as evidence, it's possible that the guy who called is not really the owner of this dog.

Her responding to the name Aggie is not significant to me. It all depends on the way the name is said. Our basset hound is named Sebastian, but I could call him Shirley, or Margaret Thatcher, and if I said it with a high-enough pitch in my voice, he'd react.

Also, as Laurie pointed out, it's possible, even likely, that Lucy was Vogel's dog, but that he had given it away. The guy calling could really be named Simmons, and he could be the person that Vogel gave the dog to. Maybe he also has a slight Boston accent.

A third possibility is that Beth's network let her down and

that she has misidentified the dog. Maybe she was never owned by Vogel at all; maybe she was owned by someone else, probably Simmons, and went stray.

The fourth and least likely scenario is the one that Beth is worried about; she fears that this really is Vogel, back from the supposed dead to claim his dog.

At first, second, and third glances this doesn't stand up to scrutiny. I suppose it's possible that the witnesses were wrong and that Vogel wasn't on the boat when it exploded. But there was plenty of publicity about it; it's inconceivable that he didn't know he was thought to have been killed.

Yet he said nothing about it, which means he either murdered the other two men or faked his own death, or both. So then after going to all that trouble, he'd come out of hiding for his dog? Okay, I would do it for Tara, but the chance that Vogel is as crazy as me is quite slim.

I tell all this to Beth, and Laurie chimes in with a similar point of view. Beth does not seem relieved; I'm sure that intellectually she understands our position, but she is not used to dealing with this kind of stuff.

"So what should I do?" she asks.

"We should assume the worst," Laurie says.

I'm not sure that I agree with her choice of words, since it causes Beth to literally flinch. But I'm on board with the approach. "If we're right, and the explanation is benign, then everything is fine no matter what," I say, trying to soften things a bit. "But since there is always a chance that this is really Vogel, we should prepare for that eventuality."

"How?"

"By talking to the authorities."

Beth nods nervously. "Will you do that for me?"

"I'll do it with you."

Pete Stanton and I are good friends.

That's if you go by my definition of "good friend." Most people would disagree with it, but I'm sure Pete aligns himself with my point of view.

Simply put, a good friend is someone you can comfortably hang out with, who shares at least some of your interests, who you can insult with impunity, and who, at the end of the day, is always there for you if you need him or her.

Of course, friendship can also be defined by the absence of things. A friend doesn't pry for personal information, he doesn't care what you wear, it doesn't bother him if you don't include him in everything you do, and he never, ever, ever, calls you on the phone just to chat.

Every phone call, and there are very few of them, must have a purpose, and it must be revealed right at the top. The only word allowed to precede the reason for calling is *hello.*

Pete checks all the friendship boxes, but I am not here at his office to make a social call. Pete is also captain in charge of the Homicide Division of the Paterson Police Department, and I have brought Beth with me so that she can tell him her story.

I didn't tell Pete the full purpose of the meeting when I set it up; I just said that it involved the boat explosion. That was good enough for him to agree to see us; for some reason homicide captains seem to be interested in homicides.

Pete doesn't know Beth, so I introduce them and explain to Pete how she and I know each other.

He rolls his eyes when I mention the dog connection. "What is it with you and dogs?"

"Dogs are like humans, only better in every respect," I say.

"Yeah, yeah, yeah. What does this have to do with the boat?"

I turn the floor over to Beth, and she tells Pete exactly what she told Laurie and me. He lets her go through the entire thing without interrupting or asking questions.

When she's finished, he asks, "Where did you leave it with him?"

"He's supposed to pick up Lucy, or Aggie, tomorrow. He said he will bring photographs and medical records that confirm it's her."

"Where is he picking her up?"

"At Andy's rescue, the Tara Foundation. That's where she is." Pete nods. "Good. Is Willie going to be there?"

"Not to worry," I say. "I'll be there." Pete believes that Willie, being extraordinarily tough and a karate expert, would be of more use than I would if something should go wrong. Pete's right, but it gets on my nerves.

"That's nice to hear; if the going gets rough, you can use sarcasm on him," Pete says. "What about Willie?"

"I expect he will be there as well."

"Good. So will we." Pete turns to Beth. "We'll be outside, and if you still believe it is Vogel after meeting with him, we'll come in for a chat. Maybe we'll come in anyway."

"Thank you," Beth says, clearly relieved but still nervous.

Pete smiles. "Then we're done here. Andy, can you stay behind? I want to talk to you about another matter."

Beth leaves and Pete says, "When you told me you were coming to talk about the boat explosion, I called a buddy at State Police Homicide, just to get updated."

"And?"

"And we danced around each other. He wanted to know why I was asking, and I wanted to know why he wanted to know why I was asking."

"You coming to a point anytime soon?"

"I think they are interested in Vogel."

"Interested how?"

"It's possible they wouldn't be surprised if they hear that he's alive."

"Did you tell them that we think he may be?"

He frowns. "Come on, Andy; I didn't even know that before you got here, remember?"

"Are you going to tell them now?"

"I think I'll hold off on that for now, until we see if this is meaningful."

There has long been a healthy rivalry between the local and state cops, and Pete is demonstrating that now. I'm sure he would like nothing better than to be responsible for a dramatic breakthrough in this case, without letting the state guys in on the process.

"Why are you telling me this?" On the list of people that Pete is disinclined to share information with, defense attorneys are at the very top, well above state or federal cops.

"I want you to be careful. If that is Vogel that she has been talking to, then he is either a murderer or a person that faked his own death after two of his pals were murdered. Neither of those things makes for a good character reference. And you are less equipped to handle bad guys than anyone I know."

"I'm touched by your concern."

"Hey, I'm just trying to protect you and your client."

"She's not my client; she's my friend. Retired lawyers don't have clients; otherwise they'd be called nonretired lawyers."

think I should be there," Laurie says. "Just in case."

"Just in case what? That the guy who wants his dog comes in shooting? I'll be there, Willie will be there, and Pete and some officers will be outside. We've got more people attending than the average Jets game."

We already discussed this last night, but Laurie is taking another shot at it this morning. "How about if I pretend to be someone looking to adopt a dog?"

"Laurie . . ."

"Okay. But Willie and Pete will definitely be there?"

"Yes, and I've already explained to them what's going on. You know, it's almost as if you think I can't handle myself if this turns physical."

She nods. "Almost."

I head down to the Foundation, and Beth is already there waiting for me. She's talking to Willie and Sondra, who I assume are assuring her that things will be fine. Vogel or Simmons is due in a half hour; there's no sign of Pete and his team, but I'm certain they are lying back so as to avoid scaring off Mr. Vogel.

We've looked at all available pictures of Vogel; the internet is full of them from his work as a pharmaceutical executive. Unless he is in a serious disguise, if it's him, we'll know it.

We hear a car pull up outside but don't look out the window, not wanting to appear too anxious. Willie is out in the reception area, and Beth and I are in the office. We can hear talking between the visitor and Willie; I assume he's telling Willie why he's here and asking where Beth is.

Seconds later the door opens and the two men come in. I can see and hear Beth take a deep breath, almost a gasp, and there's no doubt why. If this man is not Vogel, he is his twin.

Willie does the introductions. When Vogel hears my name and shakes my hand, he says, "I know you from somewhere."

"Eastside High School? Were you at the senior prom?"

He ignores that. "You're the lawyer. I've seen you on TV."

I've been interviewed on television quite a few times on legal matters, including my own cases. That's obviously where he's remembering me from.

He continues, his guard up. "What are you doing here?"

"Lawyering was just a hobby. Willie and I run this place."

He nods, probably not fully convinced. "Where's Aggie?"

"You mean Lucy?" Willie asks. "I'll get her."

While we're waiting, Vogel says, "I never thought I'd see her again."

Willie comes in with Lucy, who takes one look at Vogel and goes nuts. Absolutely nuts. She runs and jumps on him and they roll on the floor. He's petting and laughing, and she's barking and trying so hard to get close to him that there's a danger she will go through him.

If he wasn't a murder victim, this would be a poignant reunion. In fact, it sort of is anyway.

Finally, when he gets to his feet, he says, with a big smile on his face, "This is Aggie."

Beth nods. "So I see. No photographs or paperwork will be necessary, will they, Andy?"

"No, they won't. Beth, you should send the text."

Vogel is immediately on alert. "What kind of text?"

I can see Willie go on alert in case he's needed to intervene.

"We know your name is not Simmons," I say. "You're Alex Vogel, and you were believed to have died in an explosion at sea. The police are on the way in here."

"No, you don't understand. You—"

I interrupt, "Which part don't we understand?"

He starts to answer, then sort of sags at the realization that there is no immediate way out of this. "I haven't done anything wrong."

"Then you're fine."

"What about Aggie?"

"What about her?"

"If they take me in, what will happen to her?"

Before I can answer, Pete and two other officers come in. "Mr. Vogel, my name is Captain Pete Stanton, Homicide Division. You need to come down to the station with us and answer some questions."

Vogel hesitates, unsure what to do. "I don't want to. I want to take my dog and leave." He looks at Aggie, who doesn't argue the point.

"Your dog will be fine. Come with us."

Vogel turns to me. "Do I have to go with them?"

I ask Pete, "Is he under arrest?"

Pete's eyes widen at the question; I think there is a chance that he is going to shoot me. "He is coming in for questioning," he says, evading the question a bit.

"You do not have to go," I say to Vogel. "It's up to you."

I think Pete's head is going to explode. "Are you his lawyer?"

"I'm his adviser."

Pete turns back to Vogel. "If you take his advice, you're only digging the hole deeper."

"I'm taking his advice," Vogel says.

Pete gives me one final death stare before he and the other officers leave.

Once they do, Vogel says, "Thank you." Then, "I'm innocent. There's an explanation for everything."

I nod. "There'd better be, because this isn't ending here."

"I hear you. Thanks for the advice; got any more?"

"Stay nearby. They'll be coming to talk to you again, and there's no sense pissing them off; they'll find you anyway. And if you have a compelling story to tell, you might as well tell it. But with a lawyer present; only with a lawyer present."

"Like you."

"Like me, only someone else. I'm not taking on clients."

"I've got money."

"Join the club."

Dexter Wheeler badly needed a friend.

It had been three years since the auto accident that fractured, actually smashed, his hip and took him out of the workforce. Dexter had worked in a carton factory in Omaha; it was physical work and had become difficult for Dexter simply because he was aging. Once the accident happened, age was the least of his troubles.

Then came an even more troubling development: the slow erosion of his eyesight. He could still manage around his house because everything was so familiar. But tasks like shopping for food became a major challenge and were bound to get worse.

So Dexter stayed at home, venturing out only occasionally. He had no family and lived in a rural area with few neighbors. The world had forgotten Dexter, and he could do nothing about it.

Then one day a man named Allen Leary showed up at his door. He said he was from Friend in Need, an Omaha charity that helped people in situations exactly like Dexter's. They were branching out into more rural areas, had heard about Dexter's troubles, and were there to help.

Leary showed up every day; he brought food and prepared

Dexter's meals for him. They watched some television together, and Leary even helped clean up the house. They swapped some stories of their time in the service; Dexter had seen some action late in the Vietnam War, while Leary talked of his time in Desert Storm.

About a week after Leary had started coming around, Dexter became ill. At first it seemed like the flu—chills and fever and chest congestion. But then it became progressively worse, and Dexter would occasionally become delirious.

Leary took him to a hospital when Dexter began slipping in and out of consciousness. He had little idea what was happening to him, though he was aware of a doctor drawing what seemed like an unusually large amount of blood.

The doctor said that they were having difficulty culturing the bacteria, which made it harder to decide which drugs were best to target it. To be safe, the doctor was wearing what looked like a futuristic suit designed to protect him from whatever type of infection Dexter had contracted.

Leary never entered Dexter's room; the doctor told Dexter that it was prohibited because of the strong possibility of contagion. The doctor said that Leary was being updated frequently on Dexter's progress.

In Dexter's more lucid moments, he questioned the doctor why no nurses were around; the only person that ever came into the room was the doctor. The doctor explained that was also due to the danger of the infection spreading to other people; until they knew what it was, they were going to be ultra-cautious.

Dexter asked the doctor what the prognosis was, and the doctor assured him that he was going to be all right. The hospital was set up to handle just these kind of cases; they would get to the bottom of the problem and deal with it successfully.

Dexter would never realize a number of things.

This was not a hospital.

His doctor was not a doctor.

Leary was not his friend.

Dexter was very definitely not going to be all right.

Often I am unfairly maligned as lacking in courage. Nothing could be further from the truth. Courage would be my middle name had my parents named me Andy Courage Carpenter. But they didn't, and I am stuck with the reputation of being a physical coward.

That is all changing tonight. I am heading into the lion's den without a chair or whip. I am looking danger in the eye and not blinking. I am laughing in the face of imminent doom. Well, maybe not laughing—more like smiling nervously.

I am going to Charlie's Sports Bar.

Pete Stanton and I share a table with Vince Sanders, the editor of our local newspaper. I used to go there pretty much every night, but then I met Laurie, and we adopted Ricky, and . . . that ended that.

So these days I show up two or three nights a week to watch sports and eat burgers and drink beer. Charlie's is my home away from home. My home used to be my home away from Charlie's, but the balance has shifted.

It hasn't shifted for Pete and Vince. They are here every night, at our regular table, watching and eating and drinking. They don't miss me because I am not necessary for their watching and eating and drinking, and because I still pick up the entire tab, whether I am there or not.

They are already there when I arrive. Pete is the first one to see me approach the table. "Well, if it isn't the counselor for the defense. I can't believe you showed up."

"I was hungry and thirsty. Those are primary drives."

"So is the drive for revenge."

"Are you guys going to fight?" Vince asks.

"I am going to fight," Pete says. "Andy is going to die."

Vince seems concerned and turns to me. "If you're going to fight, let me hold your wallet."

I ignore that, keeping my focus on Pete. I doubt he'll go for his gun; I think he'd prefer to strangle me. "Vogel asked me if he was required to go with you. I just answered honestly."

"You could have said yes. Or you could have said nothing."

"Saying yes would have been dishonest. Saying nothing would have made me complicit in your attempt to unfairly coerce him."

"All of a sudden you're worried about honesty and fairness? You're a defense attorney!"

"An almost-retired defense attorney, and proud of it."

Our waiter walks by, and Pete stops him. "Bring me a glass of the most expensive drink you have."

"What kind of drink?" he asks.

"Doesn't matter; make it a double; and one for my friend Vince." Pete points to me. "Just put it all on his tab."

Vince sighs his relief. "Ah, back to normal. Life is good."

"Why did you do that?" Pete asks. "Really."

"In the moment I thought he was entitled to representation; he had rights and I felt he should be aware of them. And—"

Pete interrupts. "Here it comes."

"Never mind; in a million years you wouldn't understand."

"Try me."

Vince nods. "Try him."

"It was the dog. This guy was in deep trouble, the police were all over him, and he was worried about what would happen to Aggie."

Pete thinks for a moment, then nods. "For once you're right; it would take a lot more than a million years to get me to understand that bullshit."

The waiter brings the expensive drinks that Pete ordered. They're in a tiny glass. It's such a small amount that if Pete pours it on my head, which is very possible, I doubt I could tell my hair was wet.

Instead he downs his in one gulp, then says, "Worth every penny." And then, "It pays to buy the best."

"He says he's innocent and that there is an explanation for everything."

Pete frowns his derision. "There's a news event. Print that, Vince: 'Suspect claims innocence.' Stop the damn presses."

"This is off the record, Vince," I say.

Vince frowns. "I hate that expression."

"Where is your client now?" Pete asks.

"He's not my client. I was merely an innocent, bystanding dog rescuer."

"Well, one way or the other, he's going down, so you might as well collect your fee."

"Are you going to arrest him?"

"We'll see. But the state cops were very interested in what I had to say. I got the feeling it fit the puzzle they are working on quite neatly."

I shrug. "Not my problem."

My days are fairly predictable since my retirement.

I sleep until seven, take Tara and Sebastian for a walk in the park, come home for breakfast with Laurie and Ricky, then walk Ricky to school. It's May, so in a couple of months Ricky will be off at camp. I'll have to find something else to fill that time slot; maybe I'll work a nap into the schedule.

This morning starts out differently, and I have learned that "different" is rarely a positive. Laurie wakes me at six forty-five, and she's holding the local newspaper. She hands it to me. "Did you arrange this with Vince?"

The headline on the front page is "Alleged Murder Victim Turns Up Alive and Well."

"I can't believe he did this. I told him it was off-the-record. He knows that everything we say at Charlie's is off-the-record."

"So you talked about it last night?"

"Yes. Pete was rather agitated. But I specifically told Vince—"

The phone rings, and Laurie answers it. "He's right here." She hands me the phone. "It's your favorite newspaperman."

"I'm listening, Vince" is all I say.

"I know you're pissed. But I didn't quote you and I didn't use anything that you said."

"The conversation was off-the-record."

"And I kept it that way, Andy. After you left, Pete told me everything that happened and said I could run the story. It had nothing to do with you. I kept you out of it; it was all from him."

"You should have told me."

"I probably should have. But it was late when we got out of there, and I had to hurry to get the story in. You couldn't have killed it anyway because you really weren't involved. I was hoping to get to you this morning before you saw it, but clearly that didn't work out."

"I'm still pissed, Vince."

"Won't-keep-paying-the-tab pissed, or soon-you'll-get-over-it pissed?"

"Good-bye, Vince." I hang up the phone. Let him worry where his next burger is coming from.

As I'm getting off, Laurie is coming back into the bedroom. "Cable news channels are picking it up."

"Damn."

"Why are you so upset?"

I can tell it's a good question because I have no answer for it. "I don't know. Maybe it's because I don't want to have a role in whatever the hell is going on, and this makes me feel like a part of it."

Of course Laurie takes a calmer view. "At the end of the day, this story running is not going to wind up a key factor. It was eventually going to come out that Vogel is alive, and the police are going to get to the bottom of what happened. The most this might do is speed things up a bit, but even that is not likely."

I spend a few minutes watching CNN, and sure enough they have picked up Vince's story and are running with it. Murders are not such a big deal in the eyes of the media, but murder victims who come back from the dead make for a hot story.

Tara and Sebastian seem unconcerned by the developments; they just want to go for their walk in the park. I'm happy to oblige; I enjoy the walks almost as much as they do. I also do some of my best thinking while we casually stroll through Eastside Park.

Self-reflection has never been a specialty of mine, but I try to do some on the walk. What I come up with actually surprises me:

I'm curious.

While I want no part of this or any other case, I have to admit, at least to myself, that I am wondering what Vogel's story is. A successful executive goes out on a boat with two colleagues, blows the thing up, murders both of them, and fakes his own death?

Why would he do that? There could be a number of motives for murder, and almost as many for faking his death, but both?

I know nothing about the case, so I can't come close to answering those questions, but I'm curious. Not the kind of curious that would make me represent Vogel; not that strong. But I would like to know.

I liked Vogel during the brief time we were together. Whatever the reason was for his doing what he did, he came out of hiding because he loved his dog. Two points for him, and another two for being concerned about what would happen to Aggie if the police took him into custody.

That amounts to a four-point play under pressure. Not bad at all.

I fully understand that someone could love a dog and still be a murderer. But for him to take the risk that he did, well, that is some serious dog love.

It just makes me even more curious.

The state police arrested Alex Vogel at 3:34 this afternoon. An enterprising local reporter who covers northern New Jersey for the NBC affiliate in New York had a camera crew on hand when the state police showed up at the house that Vogel was renting in Ridgewood.

No mention was made as to how he knew where Vogel was staying, whether an arrest was imminent, or when exactly it would happen. Clearly, a leak came from somewhere in the law enforcement operation; perhaps they thought it would look good for people to see them acting quickly and decisively.

The reporter had a brief interview with the public relations spokesman for the state police, who said that the publicity that morning about Vogel's actually being alive had nothing to do with the timing of the arrest. The camera only showed the spokesman's head and upper body, but I have no doubt that had they scanned lower, it would have shown that his pants were actually on fire.

I'm sure that the police had been following Vogel ever since he showed up at the Tara Foundation, and maybe long before that. Pete indicated that his feeling from his phone call to them was that they seemed not surprised that Vogel might be alive.

They were certainly building their case, with no particular

pressure to make a move until they were positive that they were ready. But when the public learned that Vogel was alive, that pressure was ratcheted up enormously.

Additionally, his knowledge that the police knew about his survival made him a serious flight risk. If he could fake his death and disappear once, albeit unsuccessfully, he could clearly attempt to disappear again. That is especially true since he apparently has financial resources at his disposal.

I'm assuming that the police have been gathering evidence all along. That Vogel is alive is not enough to justify his arrest. Even though the media and the authorities identified him as having likely died in the explosion, he was under no legal obligation to come forward and tell them that they were wrong.

Simply disappearing, or not correcting faulty media information, is not a crime. Murder, on the other hand, is definitely a crime, and the reports are that Vogel was arrested for a double homicide.

He told me that he had an explanation for everything. There'd better be, or he is in deep trouble.

Laurie has been out buying camp clothes with Ricky. Based on the number of shopping bags they tote in, I feel bad for the other kids who will be in his bunk. If they haven't gone shopping yet, they are going to be upset to find that no clothes are left in the stores.

Laurie and I decide we'll talk about the Vogel situation tonight after dinner, when Ricky is in bed. We try not to discuss murders in front of him, though on occasions he has overheard us. It makes for some uncomfortable questions, which I invariably let Laurie deal with.

While I'm taking Tara and Sebastian for our pre-dinner walk, I realize I have forgotten about one other important issue . . . Aggie. It would be normal procedure when an arrest like this is made that a suspect's dog or cat would be taken to the county shelter, where he or she would be housed until the resolution of the case.

Since cases take a long time to be resolved in the quickest of circumstances, that would likely mean that Aggie would be in a cage at the shelter for months. There are two words for that: No. Chance.

I cut the walk a little short because I want to get back home and start to deal with this. Tara and Sebastian don't seem to mind; maybe they sense that their sacrifice is going toward the greater goal of helping one of their own kind.

When we get back, Laurie tells me that Beth Morris called and wants me to call her back. I decide to do so first, since she might have some information on Aggie's whereabouts.

She does.

"Aggie is at the Passaic County Shelter." She's obviously upset about it. "I went down there, but they said they can't let me have her. I asked for how long, and they said until the legal stuff was worked out."

"Who did you speak to?"

"The shelter director . . . I think his name is Brandenberger."

"I know him very well. I'll take care of it."

"You can get her out?"

"Yes."

"How?"

"Whatever it takes. At gunpoint if necessary. How did you find out where she is?"

Beth hesitates for a few moments. "Alex Vogel called me."

"After he was arrested?"

"Yes. If it's true that they really only get one phone call, he used it to call me. They had told him where they were taking Aggie and he wanted me to help her."

Once again I am impressed by Vogel's care for his dog; I understand it, but a lot of people would behave differently given his circumstances.

"Don't worry about her, Beth; I'm on it."

"There's one other thing," she says, again hesitating a bit.

Uh-oh. "What is it?"

"He wants to talk to you. He asked me to try and get you to come see him."

"What did you tell him?"

"That I couldn't make any promises, but that I would convey the message."

"Consider it conveyed."

"Will you see him? I know I have absolutely no experience with these things, and I don't want to have any, but there's something about him, Andy. If he's guilty, then he deserves whatever comes to him. But if there's any chance he isn't . . ."

I'm a little annoyed at her for pressuring me like this, but I know it's coming from a good place, so I don't come down on her for it.

"I'll think about it, Beth. But no matter what happens, Aggie will be fine. I can promise you that."

Today is a two-jail day, which means it is not going to be fun-filled.

It's something of a sad commentary on my life that I have been to both of these houses of incarceration many times before. They both take some getting used to, and I'm not making much progress in that regard.

The first jail is the Passaic County Animal Shelter. While prisoners in human jails often claim to be innocent, the inmates here really are. In most cases the humans that abandoned them or carelessly let them run off are the guilty ones and should be in a cage eating cheap kibble. But they're out there running free.

Like many shelters around the country, this one is constantly overcrowded and always underfunded. It makes for a bad combination, which is why I am here so often. The Tara Foundation gets many of its dogs from here, so that we can make sure their end result is a loving home, rather than euthanasia.

Fred Brandenberger, a terrific guy in a thankless job, runs the shelter. He does everything he possibly can to make sure that every animal that comes his way leaves for a better life. Sometimes he succeeds and sometimes he doesn't. You can see the pain in his face and hear it in his voice when he fails.

"You here about Aggie?" Fred asks me when I show up.

"How'd you know?"

"Beth told me she was going to talk to you. She's pretty persuasive."

"That dog doesn't deserve to be in here."

He frowns. "Show me a dog who does."

"That's why we do what we do," I say, playing my hole card probably sooner than necessary. Fred needs us; without our intervention he would have to euthanize many more animals. He also knows that there are plenty of other shelters in New Jersey, just as overcrowded, that we could use to get dogs.

The truth is we would never abandon Fred, and down deep he knows that, but he appreciates what we do and is accommodating.

"I'm not supposed to let her out of here."

"I know. You're supposed to keep a great dog locked in a cage for months."

"Stupid, huh?" He knows how this is going to end.

"Fred, I'll take full responsibility for her and make sure she's cared for and happy. In the process it will open up a needed space for you. It's a win-win."

"And what happens if her owner gets out of jail?"

"We won't place her until it's resolved; she'll live with Willie and Sondra. They'll feed her biscuits and bonbons every night. If the owner goes free, he will get her back. If he gets convicted, we'll find her a great home. You have my word on all of it."

Fred nods. "Good enough for me. But we keep it between us, right?"

"Absolutely."

"You want to take her now?"

"Willie will be in to pick her up later this morning. I've got somewhere else to go."

"She'll be ready; I'll make sure she gets a bath."

"Thanks, Fred. You're doing the right thing."

"What am I doing here? I should have gone to law school."

I smile. "And I shouldn't have."

When I leave, I call Willie and tell him about my discussion with Fred. We've already talked about it, and he and Sondra were both happy to bring Aggie into their home. Their dog, Cash, likes it much more when he has a buddy to play with.

"How long do you think we'll have her?" Willie asks.

"Not sure, but it won't be quick. I'm heading down to the jail now, so I might get a better sense of where things stand."

"Are you going to take his case?"

"No. I'm retired."

"I've heard that before."

"But this time I mean it."

"I've also heard that before. But if you want Aggie to get back with her owner, you'll take the case."

"You sound like Laurie."

'm sure that Alex Vogel considers jail to be the worst experience of his life.

People in his situation, meaning first-timers who have never been behind bars before, always feel this way. And while their reaction is both understandable and accurate, what they don't realize is that it's a day at the beach compared to what is ahead of them.

In county jail there are things happening . . . arraignments, meetings with lawyers, preparing for trial, and so forth. There's action going on, and while the system has decided you need to be locked up, you're still going to be able to present your side of things to a jury of your peers. It gives you something to look forward to.

State prison is different; nobody is talking to you, your legal boat has sailed, and it feels like the world has forgotten you. Which, of course, it has.

I would rather go to an animal shelter a hundred times than to a human jail or prison once. I can accomplish something at an animal shelter; I can save lives just by deciding to do it. In the human version, it's much different. Yes, I can take on a client and maybe get that person acquitted, or maybe not. But there are so many variables that I can't control that I feel somewhere between ineffectual and totally helpless.

I tell the guard manning the desk that I am Vogel's attorney. It doesn't take much convincing because the guy recognizes me. I do it because it will allow us to meet in a private room, allegedly free of eavesdropping by prison authorities. Emphasis on *allegedly*.

Vogel is brought in after I'm in place. He's not in handcuffs, which is a bit unusual. Not that there is a risk of escape; I've been searched for weapons, and guards will be stationed outside the door.

"Thanks for coming," Vogel says. "I appreciate it."

"Beth said you wanted to talk to me."

"It's awful in here."

I just wait; I know he didn't ask me here to educate me on life in jail.

"Where is Aggie?" is his next question.

Still another point for Vogel on the Andy Carpenter scorecard. "She's fine; she's going to live with my partner and his wife until you're free."

"*Until* or *if?*"

"I don't have the slightest idea." I don't. The percentages say that this will not end well for him, but every case is different. It all depends on the circumstances.

"I'm sure you won't be surprised, but I wanted to see you to ask you to be my attorney."

"I'm not taking on cases. Yours or anyone else's."

"This is my life that is on the line. I am willing to beg, to pay whatever you want."

"It's not about money."

"Then what is it about? Tell me what I can do."

I'm feeling sorry for him, but not as sorry as I'd feel for myself if I took this on. "You can get yourself a good lawyer; there is no shortage of them."

"Not as good as you. I know all about you. After that meeting at your foundation, I studied your career. I thought it might come to this."

Well, he may be a cold-blooded killer, but he's a great judge of lawyers, and he loves dogs. "Lawyers don't win cases, Alex, facts win cases."

"The facts have to be on my side because I didn't do it."

Hanging over this is a feeling of guilt that I have for being at least partially responsible for his current situation. I'm the one who alerted Pete in the first place, which provided proof that Vogel was alive. Then my conversation with Pete in front of Vince caused the media coverage.

Maybe this result was inevitable, but if nothing else, I certainly sped up the process.

"Let me ask you a question. You knew everyone thought you were dead, but you stayed in hiding. You were apparently successful in doing that. But you exposed yourself to potential discovery and arrest by calling Beth to claim your dog. Why did you do that?"

"Aggie and I have been through a lot together; she saved me in a lot of ways. So I love that dog, but on some level I also owe her. She loves me as well, we're bonded in a way I never thought possible. It just didn't seem fair to deprive her of the person she loved, because none of this was her fault."

Words are about to come out of my mouth that I am going to regret, but can't seem to control. "I'll tell you what. Right now the only urgency is to get you through the arraignment. I'll handle that, and I'll come back and listen to your story. After I do, I'll either take your case or recommend lawyers for you to hire."

"That's all I can ask."

"Okay. In the meantime, if I do sign on, then at some point I'm going to have my associate visit with you. His name is Hike Lynch. I want you to tell him everything you can about your life, both at work and especially away from it. Tell him who your friends are, and your enemies. If anyone might have the slightest desire to hurt you, no matter how irrational, tell Hike about it."

"Okay."

"And just be prepared; Hike is an unusual guy. Clinically depressing is my official diagnosis."

"Is he on medication for it? There are some outstanding anti-depressants on the market; I've worked on some of them."

I shake my head. "He's not depressed; he's depressing. You'll see what I mean; after an hour with him you'll be begging for those drugs."

Vogel smiles. "Okay. I'll be on the alert."

"And other than Hike, do not talk to anyone about anything having to do with your situation. No one. You got that?"

"I've got it."

"Good. Get some rest. You'll need it."

think you handled it just right," Laurie says.

With those seven simple words, spoken after I described my meeting with Alex Vogel, she has confirmed my view that I handled it all wrong. Laurie and I have different views of my work situation; she thinks I should have one, and I don't.

She continues, "You're helping him for now, but you've left yourself an out, based on what you learn. That's open-minded and mature."

"You don't understand; the beauty of retirement is that it is a permanent situation. It's not something to go in and out of. I'm not Brett Favre or Michael Jordan. There's no reason to leave myself an out, because I'm not in."

"Our differences are semantic. You consider yourself retired; I see it as semiretired. I think you should come around to my point of view; that way you avoid disappointment."

"How is that?"

"Well, if you're retired, then taking a case blows the whole thing out of the water. But if you're semiretired, then it fits right in. You won't feel like you failed at retirement. You'll be a success at semiretirement."

"I'm guessing you think I should take the case."

"I already know you're going to take it. I'm being supportive of your decision."

She might be right. If I wasn't thinking of taking it, I should have told that to Vogel straight out. He deserves an answer and he needs a lawyer.

But never let it be said that Andy Carpenter will ever admit that he's wrong about anything. "You can't possibly know what I'm going to do. I don't even know what I'm going to do, and I'm the one that might or might not do it."

"Andy, I'm going to give it to you straight. You like being a lawyer, even though you won't admit it. Maybe not the nuts-and-bolts part, but you like the challenge, and the strategy, and even the risk. Maybe especially the risk; it's your version of bungee jumping.

"And when you're in court, you get to be badgering and sarcastic and obnoxious, all the things that you love, but that polite society frowns on. And to top it off, you're good at lawyering, way too good for it to be something you hate deep down."

"Do you know how many weeks and months of intense work I'm taking on every time I say yes?"

"I do."

"It would mean putting everything else on hold."

"Like what?"

I was afraid she was going to ask that. "Well, take this week, for example. I was going to get the car washed, I need a new phone charger, and Tara and Sebastian could use a grooming."

"Wow, you have a full life."

"Exactly. I'm already burning the candle from both ends."

I leave the room, which is pretty much the only way I am going to get the last word. I go to my desk and turn on my computer, first checking my emails. There is nothing of importance in them; there never is. I'm not much of an emailer.

While I agree that computers have added significantly and often positively to modern life, none of that makes up for the fact that, without technology, emojis would not exist. I absolutely hate emojis; they are tiny little irritants, and in most cases I can't even figure out what they are.

I don't know why I even look at them because they add absolutely nothing to the discourse. And don't get me started on *LOL;* I can go a week without physically hearing anyone laugh out loud, but if you go by emails and texts, people spend all their time roaring with hilarity.

And recently I found out what *ROTFLMAO* means; a soon-to-be-former friend included it in an email in which they were forwarding a joke. It means "rolling on the floor laughing my ass off." Really? Then how were you typing? And the joke wasn't even funny!

Next I google all the news stories I can find about the boat explosion. Initially, and up until this week, three men were believed to have been on the boat, all deceased. In addition to Alex Vogel, the victims were Stephen Mellman and Robert Giarrusso. All three men were executives at Pharmacon, which seems to be a midlevel drug company.

There was obviously a burst of media coverage when the event happened, and at the time it was thought to have been a tragic accident. Then another flurry of stories, almost as large, appeared after word got out that the deaths were classified as homicides. No information was released as to why the change was made.

Then coverage had died down, deprived of the oxygen of new information, until this week with the revelation that Alex Vogel was alive. Quickly following on the heels of this was his arrest, which is where we are now.

If I want to find out what the reasons are for the cops thinking that Vogel did it, I can easily do so. All I have to do is take the case and read the discovery.

But that's their side of the story; Vogel says he has his own side, that there is an explanation for everything.

I'll find that out tomorrow.

Vogel's case has been assigned to the Passaic County judicial system.

The homicides, if that's what they were, took place in international waters, so technically he could be tried anywhere. But he was arrested in Paterson, which is in Passaic County, so the logical move was to try him here.

I suspect that its being convenient to my home and office did not figure into their thinking when assigning the case.

I get to the courthouse about an hour before the arraignment because I want some time to speak to Vogel. He's not here yet, so I head down to the cafeteria for some coffee. It comes out of a machine and, depending on the day, tastes like either kerosene or shit-flavored water.

I'm in luck; today's a kerosene day.

"Andy, didn't expect to see you here."

I turn and see Norman Trell, one of the better prosecutors in the county. He's not in any way brilliant, and no future law school students are going to study his trial tactics, but he's incredibly diligent. He treats every fact, no matter how obscure, as crucial. That way he is never surprised, and he is certainly never outworked.

"Yet here I am," I say, as he gets his own coffee.

"I heard you were retired."

I nod. "I heard the same thing." I try to keep the wistful tone out of my voice, but I think it comes through.

"You on a case?"

"I'm handling the arraignment for Vogel."

"I'm prosecuting. What do you mean, 'handling the arraignment'? That's all?"

"It's a work in progress."

"If you're in the market for unsolicited advice, this case might not be the one to come out of retirement for."

"Why not?"

"Because even with all your genius, it's a loser." He takes a sip of his coffee. He makes a face showing his distaste. "This tastes like shit."

"Really? I was thinking kerosene."

I head back upstairs, and Vogel is waiting for me in an anteroom. First I tell him what is going to happen once we get inside the courtroom. The prosecution will detail the charges, the judge will ask Vogel how he pleads, and assuming it's not guilty, he may or may not set a trial date.

"Not guilty," Vogel says firmly and with conviction.

"Okay. Say it just that way when he asks you, but throw a 'Your Honor' on the end of it. Now tell me what happened that day. Tell me the absolute truth. If I take this case and then find out that you lied to me, about anything, I will withdraw and you will be toast. I cannot reveal anything you say to me without your permission, so let it rip."

He nods. "How much do you know so far?"

"Just what was in the papers. You went out on your boat with two colleagues and the boat blew up. It was ruled a triple homicide, but your being here turns it into a ground rule double."

"I was on the boat, but not when it blew up . . . obviously."

"Start from the beginning."

He nods and takes a deep breath, as if preparing for an ordeal. "There were two guys that I worked with, Stephen Mellman and Rob Giarrusso. . . . I wouldn't call them friends, but we were together at Pharmacon for a good amount of time. They were already at the pier when I got to it that morning.

"We would occasionally conduct meetings there. Well, the first few meetings were in March, before the boat was in the water, so we would go to a restaurant. But the boat was better because we didn't want to be overheard."

"Why were you meeting?" I need to move this along; we're going to be called into court in a few minutes.

"We were going to start our own company. Robert was a bio-chemist, brilliant actually. Stephen was in finance; he was going to raise the money. My specialty is research and development, emphasis on research. So I would be in charge of testing new products and bringing them to market."

"You had a new product in mind?"

Vogel nods. "Yes. Companies like the one we were going to form, start-ups in this industry, can easily live or die on one product. Robert had a brilliant idea; we thought it could be huge. You want to know the kind of drug?"

"I do, but not now; we only have a couple of minutes. Tell me what happened that day."

"We were out on my boat, maybe two hours out, and we saw another boat approaching. Smaller than mine, maybe thirty-five feet. We didn't think much of it; they were still fairly far away and there was no indication it would come straight for us. That wouldn't make sense. It was a boat I don't think I had seen before.

"We had finished our meeting and were having a few beers before we were going to head back. I was going down below to get something, maybe more beer or chips . . . I don't remember. I heard these noises; they sounded like two clapping sounds. I didn't know where they were coming from; the water can carry sounds and amplify them.

"I yelled upstairs to ask the guys what the noises were, but they didn't answer. I started up the steps and I saw them; they were lying on the deck. . . . It was horrible. The only way I can describe it is that their torsos were shattered; they were in distorted positions and there was blood everywhere. I will never forget it as long as I live.

"I didn't know what to do. My assumption was that the people on the approaching boat had shot them, so I didn't want to go up where I would be a target. I couldn't get up top to the radio to send a distress signal, and there wouldn't have been time for help to arrive anyway.

"It seemed like a long time, but it was probably just a couple of minutes before I felt the impact of their boat pulling up alongside ours, and I heard them come on the deck."

"How many were there?"

"I think two; at least I only heard two voices. But I can't be sure. I heard one of them say, 'This one could be Vogel; I can't tell.'"

"So they were looking for you?"

He nods. "I couldn't think of any other explanation, then or now. One of them said that they should search the rest of the boat, that he had been told there would be three on board. So they started to come down the stairs. There is a compartment under the bed, for storage, and I hid in there. I was sure they would find me; the area to search was not that big. I never felt panic like that."

"But they didn't find you?"

He shakes his head. "They didn't look very hard. One of them said it didn't matter; once they detonated the charge, nobody would survive anyway. So they left, and I heard them disembark and their boat pull away.

"I went up onto the deck; I was literally stepping in my friends' blood. I decided I had to leave the boat; I couldn't find the explosive device that they talked about, and I assumed it could go off any second. There was a dinghy alongside the boat; it had a motor on it. I jumped into it and left. I was probably a mile away when I heard the explosion. I actually felt it."

"Do you know who the men were?"

"No, but I got a quick look at one of them. I think I would recognize him again. And I think I know who sent them."

There's a knock on the door; it opens and the bailiff says, "Andy, they're ready for you. The judge is about to come in."

I nod and turn to Vogel. "Hold that thought."

Judge Daniel Mahomes is handling the arraignment.

He's a competent judge, but completely devoid of personality. Or maybe he just hides any personality from lawyers; I've sat at his table at two charity dinners and have found it impossible to engage him in any meaningful, or even meaningless, conversation.

I asked him if he was related to Patrick Mahomes, the great young quarterback for the Kansas City Chiefs. The judge looked at me blankly, waited about six or seven seconds, then said, "No." The guy is a barrel of laughs.

There's no guarantee that Mahomes will handle the actual trial; that will depend on his schedule and caseload. Based on my experience, I think it will probably be him, but there's no way to know for sure, and it probably doesn't even matter that much. There isn't a judge on the planet who likes me.

Norman Trell and two backup lawyers are at the prosecution table; at the defense table are just me and Vogel. I didn't call in the other lawyer in my firm, Hike Lynch, because it was completely unnecessary for this purpose.

Everything that will happen today is predetermined. The only question that nobody on the other side can be sure about is how Vogel will plead. But in reality that holds little suspense;

even if a defendant is ultimately going to plead it out, they will almost invariably go with a "not guilty" at this stage. Then negotiations can follow.

Trell describes the circumstances of the case and the charges against Vogel. The prosecution has decided that the homicides were premeditated, a pretty easy call to make when explosives were planted and detonated. For that reason, they are charging Vogel with two counts of murder in the first degree.

If Vogel is convicted, he will never again have to worry about buying sunscreen.

When it comes time to plead, Vogel and I stand and he delivers his "Not guilty, Your Honor" in a steady voice. I request that bail be granted, which causes Trell to get up out of his seat.

"Your Honor, the defendant has already faked his own death and gone into hiding. He also has significant financial resources. He is the textbook definition of a flight risk."

I argue the point and offer alternatives, like a large bond, home confinement with an electronic ankle monitor, and surrender of his passport. None of it has a chance in hell of success; two counts of murder one means confinement in 100 percent of cases.

Judge Mahomes dismissively rules against us. I had alerted Vogel to how this would go, so I'm sure he's not surprised. I'm also sure he's disappointed; there's always hope until there isn't anymore.

The bailiff comes to take him away. I tell him I'll see him tomorrow to hear the remainder of his story.

He nods. "Thank you." Then, "I need you, Andy."

Not until I start to leave the courtroom do I see that Laurie has been sitting in the gallery. "I was in the neighborhood and I thought, 'Maybe I'll drop in on Andy and see what he's up to,'" she says. "Cup of coffee?"

We walk a block to a coffee shop where I frequently have

lunch during trial days. Once we're seated, Laurie says, "I'm sorry I came down so hard on you. You can live your life any way you want; you've earned it. I don't want you to feel guilty or unproductive."

"Yet I feel guilty and unproductive."

She smiles. "Good; that was my plan. Are you going to take the case?"

"I still haven't decided; I need to hear more." I then lay out for her what Vogel has told me so far. I'm not breaking lawyer-client confidentiality by doing so because Laurie is my investigator and is therefore part of the legal team.

"So he hasn't explained why he didn't get to shore and call the police?"

"Not yet."

"Did you believe what he told you so far?"

"I didn't disbelieve it. It had the ring of truth. It also had the ring of false."

"You have to decide one way or the other very soon. He's entitled to know who his lawyer is."

"I know. I'm going to hear the rest of the story tomorrow and then decide."

"Is the dog . . . Aggie . . . a factor? His relationship with her?"

"Why do you ask that?"

"Because I know you. You have this weird attitude that people who love dogs are inherently good. But that isn't true; it's possible for bad people to love dogs." She smiles. "There's a name for them. Dog-loving bad people."

"I know, but you didn't see the way Aggie reacted to him. She went nuts. Dogs are really good judges of character."

"You're insane . . . in a charming way."

"I am aware of that. It's a blessing and a curse."

Her name is Carla D'Antoni. We went out a bunch of times," he says. "I thought the relationship was getting serious. But she was secretive about things. For example, she told me I could never pick her up at her house."

Vogel is telling me who he thinks might have killed his friends on the boat. It's already not going in a direction anything like what I expected . . . and I had no idea what to expect.

"I'm not that experienced in things like this. I was married when I was twenty-two; we tried for a while to make a go of it, but it ended. Since then I hadn't seriously dated anyone until Carla. But eventually I became suspicious; I thought maybe she was married, or that she had another boyfriend."

The light goes off in my dim brain. "Carla D'Antoni."

He nods. "Exactly. Believe it or not, I didn't know who her boyfriend was until after the newspapers reported on her death."

Organized crime in northern New Jersey has become rather disorganized in the last few years. That is a natural result of a tendency for its leaders to either wind up in jail or dead. I've been involved in a number of cases that have led to some of those results.

The most recent tentative top guy is Joseph Russo, Jr., who inherited the mantle from his father, not surprisingly named

Joseph Russo, Sr. The elder Mr. Russo got his head blown off, leaving him ill-equipped to handle the job.

Carla D'Antoni was rumored to be Junior's girlfriend. Unfortunately, almost four weeks ago she suffered the same fate as the man who would have been her future father-in-law. She was murdered.

Carla was found on the cement next to a four-story warehouse in downtown Paterson in the early-morning hours. Based on her fatal injuries, she had obviously fallen from the roof of the building. No one believes she jumped.

The police have apparently made no progress in apprehending the killer. Three theories have been speculated about. One is that she was killed by an enemy of Russo's, to send a message. Another is that she did something to piss Russo off, causing him to send her his own message. The third is that Russo had nothing to do with the murder.

My view of theories is that when there are three of them, it means that the person holding them doesn't have a clue as to what he or she is talking about.

But Alex Vogel seems to be telling me that he is the one who pissed Russo off. "So you think Russo sent those guys onto the boat?"

"I can't think of any other possibilities. Carla must have told him about us, or he found out somehow and decided to take revenge on both of us."

"Why didn't you go to the police after your friends were killed?"

"I thought about it, and I might have eventually. But what was I going to tell them? That I went out with Russo's girlfriend? That's not evidence they could use to arrest him. So they'd listen and send me home. It's not like they would put me in the witness protection program. Russo would have had no trouble getting to me."

"But you have no way of knowing for sure why she was killed, or who killed her."

"That was true until those guys showed up on the boat. That ended any doubt in my mind. When she died and I read that she was involved with Russo, I didn't know who killed her or why. But the boat . . . that made me realize that he must have known about us. He was going to do to me what he did to her.

"So I was hiding until I could figure out what to do. I never did come up with a strategy."

As a professional with considerable experience dealing with criminal activities like murder, I consider this story total horseshit. And that might be understating the case.

"I think you are completely misjudging this," I say.

"What do you mean?"

"Guys like Russo don't send boats out on the ocean to commit murders. They don't board boats on the open seas; they're mobsters, not pirates. That's not how this works. If they wanted to kill you, they would wait at the pier and put a bullet in your head. Or when you got in your car to go home, you'd step on the gas and wind up as a cream sauce on the parking lot."

"It can't be anyone else."

"Why not?"

"Because I'm an executive in a corporation; the most dangerous thing I do all day is have one too many drinks at lunch. I don't know killers, I don't hang out with them, and I don't give them reason to kill me."

"And you're sure they were looking for you?"

"Positive. They said my name; they wondered if I was one of the ones they shot. And they were going to look further for me; then they decided if by any chance I was on the boat and alive, the explosion would kill me. There's no doubt about it; I was the target." Then, more softly, "And I was the only one who lived."

"Was there anything of value on the boat that they might have stolen?"

He shakes his head. "I didn't do an inventory; I was too anxious to get out of there. But there was nothing that was worth much, other than the boat itself. Certainly nothing that would justify or explain murder."

I'm fairly sure that Vogel is wrong about Russo's involvement, but that doesn't mean I think he's lying. It makes sense that he believes it, but he likely has no experience dealing with Russo or people like him.

Unfortunately, I do; it's among the reasons I am on this endless journey toward retirement.

The story about the events on the boat, in Vogel's telling, rings true. I can see why, believing what he did about Russo, that he panicked and hid. It was simultaneously stupid and logical.

"Why did you leave the island to rent a car on the mainland? There were car rental places on the island. The police believe it was so you would be harder to trace."

He shakes his head. "It had nothing to do with the police. I thought Russo's people might still be on the island looking for me. So I hitched a ride and got out of there as fast as I could."

I don't claim to know when someone is lying; my success rate in judging the veracity of people ranges from 49 to 51 percent. So I go with my gut, even though my gut is no better at it than I am.

One other new factor impacts whether I take on Vogel as a client. The media is already reporting that I am his attorney, based on my handling the arraignment. I understand why they have made the assumption, even though it is currently technically incorrect.

If I drop him now, it will seem as if I am making a judgment on his case and could be interpreted negatively by the general public, of which the future jurors are a part.

But that is a secondary consideration. More important is that both my head and gut say that Vogel is telling the truth. Not only that, but he loves dogs.

"I'll take your case," I say.

Unfortunately, the media's reporting my being Vogel's attorney has had another negative repercussion.

It's alerted my team that we are taking on a client. In most situations that wouldn't matter; legal teams expect to have clients and are prepared for it. My squad? Not so much, so I have to break it to them carefully.

First there is Edna, my office manager. She is able to do her job efficiently because none of us ever go to the office. That enables her to manage it at her leisure, and leisure is Edna's strong point.

Edna will hate the idea of my taking on a client, although since she never does any work, she will be the least affected. She'll still find time to cash her weekly checks and do her crossword puzzles.

She makes me look driven.

Hike, the only other lawyer in what I euphemistically call a "firm," will have mixed feelings. He'll want the money, and the work won't bother him, but he'll hate being involved in a losing effort. Hike's a pessimist and there is no potential effort that he doesn't see as a losing one. I'm just glad that Hike is on the defense team and not the jury.

Sam Willis will be thrilled, but as always his enthusiasm will need to be tempered. Sam is my accountant, but on our legal adventures he serves as our computer guy. By that I mean that he is a hacker supreme, capable of sneaking into any computer anywhere. Almost none of it is legal, and the good thing about Sam is that he cares about that even less than I do.

But Sam sees himself as more than the sum of his keyboards; he wants to be in on the action. His constant refrain is that he wants to "hit the streets," doing stakeouts or shoot-outs. My preference would be cookouts, make-outs, and dropouts.

The rest of my team is a contained unit. My wife, Laurie, a former cop herself, has joined up with another former cop, Corey Douglas, and Marcus Clark to form what they call the K Team. The name recognizes their fourth member, a former police German shepherd named Simon Garfunkel. Simon has been Corey's partner for a long time.

They are an effective group, and Marcus is particularly effective. He is the toughest, scariest human in this or any other galaxy. He has saved my life on numerous occasions; the only negative effect of that is that I remain alive and therefore capable of taking on new clients.

Willie Miller is also here. Willie isn't technically a part of the team, but as an ex-client of mine and my current partner in the Tara Foundation, Willie is a friend who cares about me. Since he is the toughest person I know, other than the aforementioned Marcus, Willie is on occasion able to demonstrate that caring by also serving as my protector.

Willie has also saved my life on occasion, as has Laurie, and even Simon Garfunkel. It annoys me that I have never successfully saved my own life, unless you include stuff like looking both ways before I cross the street, and washing fruit before I eat it.

As an obnoxious defense attorney who frequently pisses off dangerous people, I tend to need a lot of protecting.

We start every case with a team meeting at which I tell everyone what we know so far about the case we are starting. Since we're by definition at square one at that stage, I rarely have much information to impart. I just want to get everybody focused and on the same page.

Right now we're meeting in my office, which is on the second floor above a fruit market on Van Houten Street. If you are a lawyer trying to impress potential clients, this isn't the kind of office you would bring them to.

The place is, to put it kindly, something of a dump. On the other hand, the big, fancy firms don't have the sweet aroma of fresh cantaloupe wafting through their open windows.

I'm a fan of old TV sitcoms, and in one *Honeymooners* episode, Norton is able to tell what time it is by when the aroma of egg foo yong reaches his apartment window from the Chinese restaurant downstairs. He's done this by having figured out the precise speed at which egg-foo-yong aroma rises.

Cantaloupe is a little slower, but the sweet smell has just reached us, so I can tell without looking at my watch that it's ten after ten, since the stand opens at ten. That makes it five minutes to watermelon.

"I know you have learned from media reports that we have a client. I didn't contact you all personally because those reports were premature, though ultimately accurate. We do now have a client."

There is a soft but audible moan from Edna.

"Edna, is something wrong?"

"No. I just didn't expect a new client so soon. Or ever. It's an adjustment."

"I feel your pain."

With that I address the group. "Our client, as you've read, is Alex Vogel. He is wrongly accused of having murdered two colleagues by blowing up his boat."

Hike frowns at my "wrongly accused" assertion, but refrains from snorting or moaning. The interesting thing is that I'm pretty sure he is not the only person in the room who assumes Vogel's guilt. The natural inclination of both Laurie and Corey Douglas, as former cops, is to believe that arrests are generally made for good reason.

They recognize the possibility that the accused is innocent, but consider it unlikely. The truth is that they are right more often than not.

Laurie and I have not talked about whether she thinks Vogel is guilty of the crime since she believes he is entitled to a forceful defense either way. I have not discussed the matter with Corey at all. Along with Marcus, they will do their investigative work regardless of their personal opinion of Vogel or his guilt or innocence.

"The prosecutor is Norman Trell," I say. "Hike, please tell him that we've signed on and that we want to start receiving discovery immediately."

Hike nods. "That is not going to make for fun reading."

"I don't know much, other than Vogel's side of the story. I've handwritten it out; Edna, please type it up and distribute it to everyone here."

The horror on Edna's face is evident. "How many pages will it be?" She cringes.

"Probably two."

"Single-space?"

"Double."

She sighs her relief. "Okay. When do you need it?"

"Hopefully before the trial." Then, "Once we read the discovery and have a plan of attack, we can give out individual assignments. Vogel has a theory about who the killers are, which you will read in Edna's perfectly typed version. Though I doubt that he's correct, it's something we'll definitely need to follow up on."

I tell them the tentative trial date, which is sooner than I'd like. Most defense attorneys like to delay as much as possible. I differ on that. Our client is in jail; he is currently being punished for a crime we are hoping to prove he did not commit.

I would of course be opposed to a trial before we are ready, but we can generally be fully prepared well before a trial date is reached. So if we're ready, we might as well move forward. If we find we need more time, judges are likely to grant it.

I continue, "The undisputed facts are that he went out on the boat with the two victims, the boat blew up, but Vogel survived. He also went into hiding and did nothing to correct the belief of the police and public that he had died in the explosion.

"My guess is that the prosecution has more than that going for them, but we'll know that soon enough.

"That's all for now."

t will take twenty-four hours to get the initial discovery documents.

That doesn't represent a deliberate delay by the prosecution; it just takes time to cull through the material, decide what is necessary to turn over, and make copies for us. I might be suspicious of certain prosecutors, but Norman Trell isn't one of them. He's always been a straight shooter with me.

We can't do much until then, since it is always helpful to have that information before we start investigating; it helps put things into context. Usually Laurie and I take this time to check out the murder scene, but that's not possible here.

The homicides for which Vogel is charged took place out on the ocean. Even if we could figure out exactly where, it wouldn't matter. Water is water, and my guess is that the fish will be tight-lipped about what they witnessed.

So instead we go to the pier where the boat originated. It's a long drive for us, almost two hours, so we drop Ricky off at Will Rubenstein's house. That will give them a chance to plan their bungee-jumping outing with Will's father, Brian.

It should come as a surprise to no one that Long Beach Island is an island, but the good news is that one can get there by car on a causeway. The causeway is perpendicular to the island itself, and once you cross it, a series of small towns are to both the left and the right.

In general terms, the island gets less commercial, and the houses more expensive, the further to the left one goes. The pier where Vogel's boat was docked was in Beach Haven, which is to the right off the causeway.

Probably fifty boats are docked in the area. We head for the office of the pier manager. He's not in, but an assistant is manning the desk. We introduce ourselves and she tells us her name is Dina. She doesn't give us a last name, which at this point is not terribly important. And maybe she's known by just the one name, like Cher or Madonna.

We ask Dina if she was on duty the day that Vogel's boat went on its ill-fated trip.

"Oh, yeah. I saw them leave. Mr. Vogel even stopped in here to pay his rental fee before they left."

"Rental fee?" Laurie asks. "Is that paid in advance?"

Dina nods. "Yup. It's due the first of the month and is good for that month."

This is of some significance and makes me feel a bit better about our client. He had no reason to pay a fee for the next month if he was planning to blow up the ship that day. Of course, he might have done it to make people come to the same conclusion we are making. But on balance it's helpful.

"Was he acting strangely in any way?" I ask. "Did you notice anything unusual?"

"No. He was in a good mood, smiling and stuff. He always seemed like a nice guy."

"Did you talk with his two friends?"

She shakes her head. "No, but I saw them."

"Would other people have seen them as well?"

"Sure; this place is always crowded. The police came and talked to a lot of people, including me."

We could go around asking people if they were here that day and saw anything, but it would not be a good use of our time. We're in the dark as to who to actually talk to; the discovery documents will be a road map in that regard.

I'm sure the cops have a number of people who can testify that Vogel boarded the *Doral.* Dina was able to, and if that day was anything like today, Vogel and his friends would have been exposed to many others, as Dina said.

"I'm sure they can place him on that boat," Laurie says.

I nod. "No doubt. But the bottom line is that it doesn't matter; he was, in fact, on the boat and we are not going to argue otherwise."

"What are we going to argue?"

"Beats the hell out of me."

We head to Loveladies, a small town on the other end of the island. Vogel said he came ashore there in his dinghy. He told us he came to a small pier at a private home and left the dinghy there. It's impossible for us to know which home and which pier, so we just look around to get the lay of the land.

The cops no doubt know which house, and they certainly must have the dinghy. It will serve to help prove their case that Vogel was on the boat and bailed out.

All that's left for us to do is stop at Harvey Cedars Shellfish Company on the way back. I have the crab cakes and Laurie has a lobster roll.

Definitely the highlight of the trip.

For two people, the news that Alex Vogel was alive represented an absolute disaster.

Charlie Phillips and Orlando Bledsoe had been positive he was dead; there simply was no way he could have survived the explosion. They hadn't gone down to the bottom level of the boat because if Vogel was waiting there with a gun, they would have been sitting ducks.

So they set the charge and detonated it remotely. They knew how powerful it was and had seen the media reports afterward. None of the bodies had been recovered, and none would be.

Vogel could not be alive, unless he hadn't been on the boat in the first place.

But he was alive; that much was now certain. His mug shot was in the paper. There was no accompanying explanation for how he survived, and in truth, to Phillips and Bledsoe it didn't matter. Their fate was sealed with the news of Vogel's survival.

The worst part was that they had lied. They told their employer that Vogel was dead and had embellished the story. They were not about to say that they had feared looking for him at the bottom of the boat, so they said he was shot and killed with the others. They couldn't now claim he wasn't on the boat when they had already sworn otherwise.

When weeks had gone by with nothing to question their certainty and their story, Phillips and Bledsoe thought they were in the clear. They had made a great deal of money for the assignment, more than triple what they had ever made before. They started to spend it, living the good life.

Once the news came out, continuing to live any life at all seemed a long shot.

Their employer wouldn't come asking for an explanation because none could be acceptable. Phillips and Bledsoe were sent on a job and paid well for it. It was crucially important, and they had repeatedly claimed it was accomplished.

It wasn't accomplished.

They lied.

End of story.

They would be prepared, but it wouldn't matter. There was no way to know who was coming or when. They also had no idea where or how it would happen. Anyone they knew could be their killer, so no one could be trusted.

And because anyone and everyone represented possible danger, there was no way to go on the offense. Phillips and Bledsoe could only prepare as best they could for the inevitable, knowing it would not be enough. They could ward off one attempt, or maybe two, but their enemies would never stop coming and would ultimately succeed.

Of course, they were right.

The bodies of Charlie Phillips and Orlando Bledsoe were found in Pennington Park, each with a single bullet fired into the back of his head.

The police immediately understood that these were professional killings. As such, there were not likely to be clues to point them to the killer, and none were found.

Hike was right; I've had more fun at rectal exams than I'm having reading the discovery.

My hope had been that the prosecution's case was based on a belief that Vogel escaped from the boat and went into hiding, then didn't reveal himself even after it was publicly obvious that he was presumed dead. Such actions would certainly be taken as consciousness of guilt, and that can be damning in itself.

That will be a key theory that they will advance. Unfortunately, they have much more.

In addition to witnesses placing Vogel and his two colleagues at the pier and boarding the boat, two of the witnesses also heard a heated argument between them.

As expected, the abandoned dinghy has been found, identified as Vogel's, and confiscated. That they found it is not in itself significant; once it was known that he was on the boat, he had to get to shore somehow.

The key facts are where it was found and Vogel's actions afterward. He knows his way around the area, and the dinghy had a motor. He could have navigated it toward the pier where he kept his boat, where people would have been able to help him. Instead, he went far out of his way to land where there would be much less chance of his being seen.

Then, when one has escaped death in an explosion where two others died, the normal, innocent thing to do would be to get to a phone and call the police. Vogel, instead, seems to have gotten to a car-rental place on the mainland, where he rented a car. My guess is he hitchhiked over there, but I haven't confirmed that with him yet.

The police have all this information, plus the knowledge that car-rental offices on the island itself were open that Vogel chose not to use. That he passed them by and instead rented one from a place off the island speaks, in the minds of the police and prosecutors, to his wanting to be difficult to trace.

Laurie comes into my office while I'm reading through this, and I update her. She says, with uncharacteristic understatement, "That's pretty bad."

"You think? Because I haven't told you the worst part yet."

"Uh-oh. Let's hear it."

"Vogel was a marine; he fought in Iraq. Guess what his specialty was?"

"Munitions."

"Bingo. And guess what they found in his basement?"

"Bomb-making equipment?"

"Not quite. There were traces of explosives; military grade. The kind that was used to blow up the boat."

"This was his house where they found it, or the place he's been hiding since the explosion?" she asks.

"His house. It was broken into after the story broke about the accident. Apparently one of those ghoulish situations, where people rob the homes of the recently deceased, sometimes during their funerals. He was presumed dead by the media at the time. While the police were investigating the break-in, forensics picked up the explosive traces."

"They might have suspected all along that he planted the bomb himself. They would have considered it a possible murder-suicide, but once they found the dinghy, they would have known better."

"As bad as this is, it could have been worse," I say.

"How?"

"They could have found a signed confession, or a diary in which he promised to kill those two people and then convince Andy Carpenter to represent him."

"Maybe he has an explanation for everything."

"I'm looking forward to hearing it."

The phone rings and Laurie answers it. She listens for a moment, then says, "Yes, he's been reading them. Just a second; he's right here." She holds out the phone. "It's Hike."

Hike has been at his house reading his copies of the discovery documents. Even if an ironclad alibi for Vogel was in them, Hike would find a way to view it in a negative light.

I don't want to talk to him about it; I'm miserable enough on my own. "Tell him I'm not in."

She covers the phone. "I just told him you were right here."

"Tell him that you mistook someone else for me."

She smiles. "Who?"

"A passing, handsome stranger."

"I wish," she says wistfully. Then, "Take the phone."

I have no choice, so I do. "Hello, Hike. Feeling upbeat today?"

"Our client is going to the electric chair."

"New Jersey doesn't have an electric chair, Hike."

"If they've read through this discovery, then I'll bet they are wiring one up right now. High voltage."

"Try not to mention that to the judge during the trial."

"We're going to trial with this?" Hike makes no effort to hide his incredulousness. "The jury will be back before lunch." Then, "You must see how bad this is. Wait a minute, I am talking to Andy Carpenter, the lawyer, right?"

"Nope. This is a handsome, passing stranger."

can handle a defense in one of four ways, and this case is no exception.

One way is to not take on the client at all, but that boat has clearly, and sadly, already sailed. Or, to make it more relevant to the current situation, that boat has already exploded.

Another way is to plead it out. That is of course up to the client. He can often get a lesser sentence in return for pleading guilty and avoiding a trial. I will discuss that possibility with Vogel, though I doubt he will go for it, and I doubt the prosecution's offer will be generous. With their case, they have little reason to be.

That leaves the two real-world possibilities. One is to demonstrate conclusively that Vogel did not, in fact could not, have committed the crime.

That's going to be a tough one. Three people were on that boat, and Vogel is the only one left alive. Afterward he acted exactly as a guilty person would act. Throw in the explosives traces in his house and his arguing with the deceased, and there is not going to be a magic bullet that exonerates him.

That leaves option four, which is to find out who actually killed Mellman and Giarrusso and then set the explosive. I am not ruling out the possibility that Vogel is in fact guilty of the crime, but I accomplish nothing by going there. For the purpose of our investigation we have to operate under the assumption that he is a victim himself.

To make matters worse, in this case option four is particularly difficult. Usually we can learn a lot by studying the murder victims and figuring out who else might have wanted them dead. That doesn't work here because Vogel said the killers were looking for him.

If he's telling the truth, and again I have to take it on faith that he is, then the two victims were collateral damage. They were just on the wrong boat at the wrong time and died simply because of their connection to Vogel.

So it appears that we'll wind up needing to identify someone who had a motive for killing Vogel. I don't yet know enough to get a sense of how difficult that might be; we're just not nearly far enough into this. I doubt I'll be able to just google *real boat killer.*

For now, I've asked Sam to find out what he can about the two victims, just in case that turns out to be relevant. He's here to report to Laurie and me on that now.

My arrangement with the K Team is that Laurie will be the point person and will then be responsible for directing her teammates Corey Douglas and Marcus. If you've seen the three of them, then you'll have no trouble figuring out why I picked her.

Sam is here early because he knows that Laurie will make him pancakes; Sam has a pancake addiction. This morning he downs eight of them before wiping blueberry juice off the side of his mouth and getting started on his report:

"Victim number one is Stephen Mellman, although there's no particular order. You can call Mellman victim number one or two; doesn't really matter."

Sam can take forever to get to a point; he seems to relish it, but it drives me crazy. Laurie is usually able to take it in stride.

"You want to call him victim number one or two?"

"Sam, I don't care what order you put them in. But I can tell you this: if you don't hurry up, you are going to be victim number three."

"Okay, we'll call Mellman number one. Thirty-eight years old, married, no children, lived in Teaneck. Graduated from Tufts, MBA from Columbia, been at Pharmacon for three years. Of course, Pharmacon has only been in business for three years. Before that he was at a hedge fund."

"What did he do at Pharmacon?" Laurie asks.

"Vice president, number two in the Finance Department, under CFO Gerald Bennings. Main responsibility seems to have been raising money, attracting investors. He apparently has good connections in that world. A business like Pharmacon, a start-up in that industry, requires a lot of cash for research. They need time to get up and fully running. They have to survive until they can create successful drugs and get them to the marketplace."

"Was he good at his job?"

Sam shrugs. "Hard for me to say. They certainly raised money, but I can't say what he's responsible for. I have more background information on him; it's all in these folders."

"What about the other victim? Giarrusso?" I ask.

"Right. Victim number two," Sam says, as if we needed to confirm his identity. "Unmarried but engaged. Thirty-five years old, lived in Fort Lee. He's a special case, clearly a brilliant guy. MIT undergraduate, master's degrees from Penn in chemistry and biology, Ph.D. in chem from Stanford. I imagine he could have written his own ticket when he was ready to enter the job market."

"What was his position there?"

"Second-in-command in the product-development division. He was a key guy for new drug creation. Of the three guys on that boat, I would think he'll be the toughest to replace by far."

"Either of them have criminal records?" Laurie asks. "Any red flags?"

Sam shakes his head. "Based on the records and their bios, it could have been a Boy Scout meeting on that boat."

"Okay. Thanks, Sam."

"No problem. You know, giving this report has made me hungry."

Laurie nods. "I'll make some more pancakes."

Andy, I know you're good," Norman Trell says.

"Uh-oh . . . here it comes" is my response. He's asked me to his office to discuss the upcoming case, which means he is going to assess our interest in pleading it out.

"No, really. You're the best. But Clarence Darrow couldn't win this one."

"Of course not. Darrow's dead; haven't you heard? This past Wednesday he just keeled over at the gym. A hundred and sixty-three years old and, poof, just like that. Really puts things into perspective, doesn't it?"

"Thanks for sharing that, Andy. I'll send a card. I think you know that my point is that no one would have a shot in this case. Including you."

"Are you making an offer?"

He nods. "I am. I've been authorized to offer forty to life. No possibility of earlier parole."

"Wow. You old softy, you."

"It's the best I can do and it's better than he'll get from the judge and jury."

"He's forty-two years old," I say. "You think he should take a deal where the earliest he could get out would be when he's eighty-two?"

"He should have thought of that before he killed two people."

"Unless he didn't."

"Come on, Andy; you know the facts in this case. Forget the evidence, considerable as it is. He couldn't have acted guiltier if he wore a sandwich board with a signed confession on it."

I'm not going to argue with Trell and in the process tell him our strategy. In the first place, it would help him prepare for it at trial. In the second and even more important place, we don't have a strategy. Hopefully we'll develop one.

"I haven't talked to my client about this yet. I will, but I can't imagine he'll consider your offer. Not too many people grab at the chance to die in prison."

"He turned his friends into shark food."

"Someone did." I stand up. "This has been a rare treat. I'll get back to you."

"The offer comes off the table at close of business on Friday."

"That will give me something to look forward to."

I leave Trell's office and head down to the jail to talk to my client. It's my obligation to present Trell's offer to him, even though I don't think he should take it and can't imagine that he will.

It's not difficult for a lawyer to see his client at the Passaic County jail, especially when the client is pretrial. Lawyer visits are frequent, and over the years, when the lawyers have been forced to wait too long, they've complained pretty loudly.

As affable and pleasant as I always am, I have been one of the loudest complainers. We were finally heard, and the authorities decided it was not worth the aggravation to piss us off.

Once I confirm that Vogel is feeling okay and getting everything he needs, I tell him Trell's offer. Gleeful is not the way I would describe his response.

"That's crazy, Andy."

"It's also his best and final offer."

"Are you saying you think I should take it?"

I shake my head. "No. You'd either die in prison or come out a very old man. There's no upside in that."

"Is that why you're saying it, or is it because you think we can win?"

I'm always honest with my clients when it comes to . . . well, everything. They deserve that; it's their life that is on the line. "I have no idea whether we can win. I'm not that far into it. Nothing I've seen so far fills me with confidence, but that could change."

"What have you seen?"

"When you were getting on the boat, a witness says you were arguing with the other two guys. What was that about?"

For a moment he looks surprised and confused. "Arguing? I guess it's possible, but it would have been about business. And we wouldn't have been screaming or anything."

"What would have been the cause of a business argument?"

"We were planning to start a company, and we each had our own ideas of how and especially when to do it. We were leaving behind some money; Pharmacon was planning an IPO."

I know almost nothing about finance, but I do know that an IPO is an initial public offering, which basically means that the company goes public and sells stock to raise money. "And all three of you would have profited from it?"

He shrugs. "Yes, though not as much as I once hoped. I doubt it will go very well. But they need to do it to get financing to keep going."

"Why won't it do well?"

He hesitates. "I need to be careful in what I say because I still have an obligation to them. I'm probably still an employee, unless they've already fired me. So let's just say that the business depends on certain results and performance of their products, and . . . well, can we leave it at that?"

"Yes, we can." I sort of admire his sense of loyalty.

"The IPO was significant to us though because of more than money. Once it happened, we would have been stuck there. Part of the deal for our getting the stock was our signing noncompetes; we wouldn't have been able to leave and do anything else in that industry for at least two years. And if we left anyway and let them sue us, at a minimum we would have lost our stock, and probably much more."

"I'm going to want more information on that, but it's not necessary now." Now for a change of subject. "Did you ever work with explosives in your house?"

His response is immediate. "Explosives? Of course not."

"Traces were found there after the explosion."

For the first time I see a flash of anger. "That's impossible."

"The police forensics found it. I know the cop who was on the scene. If he says it was there, it was there."

"Then someone else put it there. My house was broken into; I read it in the paper. I don't know what was stolen; I never got to go back there. But maybe the purpose was not to take things, but to leave those traces behind. Maybe Russo."

He continues to think that Russo is behind it because he had an affair with Russo's girlfriend. But Russo would be no more likely to frame Vogel by planting traces of explosives than to send a boat out with hit men on it. Both would show way more finesse than he is capable of.

Also, if Russo was intent on killing Vogel, Russo had no reason to frame him for anything. "It's not Russo's style," I say.

"It's not my style either."

'So we're turning down the plea deal?"

"We are."

My world has few true geniuses.

To me a genius is someone who has the vision and smarts to invent something that makes my life easier and more enjoyable. Whoever came up with the idea for ESPN qualifies. As does the inventor of the point spread for gambling purposes. The TV remote control is a perfect example of inspired brilliance; walking to the television to change the channel is a nightmare I have no desire to relive.

Right at the top of the genius list is the man or woman who created chocolate-covered cherries. To take two perfect tastes like cherries and chocolate and combine them into one took an inspired intelligence I can't even aspire to.

Their invention even left room for users to indulge their personal preferences. My technique in eating them is to let the chocolate slowly dissolve, but I also respect those who immediately chew. The brilliant design allows for both approaches.

I eat in awe.

I don't know any of the other kinds of geniuses, like scientists, mathematicians, and the like, but that doesn't mean I don't respect them. Some of them might even rank up there with the chocolate-cherry guy.

I might meet some of those kind of geniuses today. I'm at

Pharmacon, where Vogel, Mellman, and Giarrusso all worked. I called Eric Buckner, whose official title is founder and CEO, told him who I was, and asked if we could meet.

He jumped at the opportunity. The Andy Carpenter celebrity opens doors.

The company is located in Paramus, just up the road from the Paramus Park mall. It's not a terribly large building, two stories and not covering much land. It's modern, all chrome and glass; the building looks like it was built about an hour ago.

About thirty parking spaces are in the lot, and it's only two-thirds filled, leading the deductive mind of Andy Carpenter to think that not a hell of a lot of people are working here. Either that or carpooling is a significant part of the company culture.

The reception area takes up a much larger area than I would have suspected after seeing the place from the outside. It's also modern and looks expensive to have put together; a lot of care went into this reception area.

I doubt they did that to impress FedEx deliverymen; it's more likely that they play host to investors. If the intent was to make a good first impression, I think they've pulled it off.

All I have to do is tell the receptionist my name and she says, "I'll tell Eric that you're here." If the receptionist refers to the CEO as Eric, I've got a feeling this is an informal work environment. It would be my kind of place, if I had the slightest bit of interest in being in any kind of work environment.

Eric Buckner comes out to greet me, and he's dressed like the kind of CEO that the receptionist could call Eric. He's wearing sneakers, jeans, and a sport shirt with the sleeves rolled halfway up his arms. He looks like he's in his late twenties, although I know from his online bio that he's thirty-four.

"Andy Carpenter? Eric Buckner." We shake hands; his shake

is firm, overly so, as if he's showing off. He also holds it a couple of seconds too long, which is a pet peeve of mine.

My philosophy is shake and end it; it's an introduction, not an intimate experience.

As we head back to his office, we pass other offices with employees dressed similarly to Buckner. Two of them actually have dogs with them, one a golden retriever.

Once we're in Buckner's office, he offers me a drink, and I take a Diet Coke. He opens with "I'm not saying this because you're representing him, but there is no way that Alex Vogel did what they are accusing him of."

This is as good a place to start as any, so I ask him why he says that.

"Because I know him, and I knew Stephen and Robert, and I knew the relationship they had. They were friends, but it wouldn't matter if they were enemies. Alex could never intentionally hurt anyone."

"What did they do here?"

"Robert was a chemist. Number two in the department on the chart, but easily the most talented. He was brilliant."

"So he worked on developing drugs?"

Buckner nods. "Yes. A major loss not only to our company, but to medicine and good health everywhere. Stephen was in finance; in our industry attracting capital and investors is a constant challenge. For us more than most."

"Why is that?"

"We're a small company, and like most of our size we depend on one breakthrough drug. Ours is going to be Loraxil."

"Going to be?"

He nods. "We haven't completed the FDA approval process, but we will, and fairly soon. It's going well. It will be one of the great advances in medicine."

"What kind of drug?"

He tells me what I already know from news reports in recent years, that bacteria are becoming increasingly resistant to conventional antibiotics, creating so-called superbugs that can't be stopped. "But Loraxil can stop them," he says with evident pride.

"If it's so great, why is it hard to get investors?"

He thinks for a moment, as if trying to figure out the best way to educate me. "Good question. Two reasons. The first, and it's a problem with all antibiotics, is that it's prescribed for a specific period of time. You have an infection, you get a ten-day regimen, and then you're done."

"So?"

"So the real money is in drugs that treat chronic illnesses. You take them forever."

"You said two reasons?"

He nods. "You're a lawyer, right?"

I reluctantly admit that I am.

"Take driverless cars. When they arrive in force, they're going to have accidents, no matter how good the technology is. It's inevitable. It will open up a whole new area of the law, trying to deal with the implications of it. Right?"

I nod my agreement. "Very likely."

"Right. But would you go out tomorrow and hire a bunch of lawyers for your firm based on their expertise in driverless-car legal issues?" He answers his own question. "Of course not, because they'd just be sitting around with nothing to do. Those cases aren't here yet."

"And your point is that those superbugs aren't here yet?"

"They're here, but pretty rare. So rare that it's hard to do human testing; we have to swoop in when we hear of a case. So our drug will be huge in the future, but to be ready for the superbug invasion, we have to develop it now.

"But who is going to buy it when the need is not great yet? You're not hiring those lawyers, and doctors and pharmacies aren't buying these drugs.

"So we have to have the financial ability to create it and bring it to market, because its time is coming. And then we'll save lives and laugh all the way to the bank."

I decide to switch subjects. "Do you know why Vogel, Mellman, and Giarrusso were meeting on that boat?"

He shrugs. "Probably planning to start their own company. Happens all the time. I once did the same thing; that's why we're sitting here."

"It wouldn't have bothered you?"

Another shrug. "They would have missed out on the IPO when we do it, but that's up to them. I would have wished them well, hired replacements, and life goes on."

"It stopped going on for Mellman and Giarrusso."

Eric frowns. "That's for sure."

"Any idea who might have wanted to hurt them? Or hurt Alex Vogel?"

Eric shakes his head. "I really don't, and I've thought about it. But I only knew those guys professionally; we didn't hang out or anything. I'm sorry to say that there could have been major things going on in their lives that I just wouldn't know about."

"I'd like to talk to some of their coworkers."

"Fine with me. I obviously can't make anyone talk to you; people are still pretty shaken up. But I'll put out the word that I approve."

"Thanks."

"Alex Vogel is a good guy; let me know if there's anything I can do to help."

Someone wanted Alex Vogel dead.

They may or may not have also been after Mellman and Giarrusso, but based on Alex's story, he was certainly a target. So our task, while difficult to accomplish, is essentially a simple one. When we find out who wanted Vogel dead, we'll know everything.

The key to finding out the "who" is to learn the "why." Something that Vogel did, or something he knew, created his enemy. To that end, Vogel has a theory. Actually, it's more than a theory. In his mind it's a certainty, and one that caused him to go into hiding.

He believes it is Joseph Russo, Jr., because of the affair Alex had with Russo's now-deceased girlfriend. I don't think that's at all likely, but it would be legal malpractice for me not to investigate it. Vogel was the target of a murderer, and he had given an actual murderer in the person of Joseph Russo, Jr., a reason to seek revenge against him.

Even though I never believe in coincidences, I think this is possibly an exception. I just don't see Russo behaving in this manner, but I would be dropping the legal ball by not checking it out. My first step in doing so is to call Willie Miller.

Willie had a weird friendship with Russo's father, Joseph

Russo, Sr., who had run the crime family until he met his un-timely demise. Willie and the senior Russo had been in prison together; Willie had been wrongly accused and convicted, while the same could very definitely not be said for Russo.

Three inmates trying to make a name for themselves had commenced an attack on Russo with makeshift knives. Willie witnessed this, decided the odds were not fair, and rushed to Russo's defense.

Willie is a good defense-rusher. By the time he was finished, the three attackers were in the prison hospital, and Russo was indebted to Willie for the relatively short rest of his life.

I have no idea if Willie knows Russo's son, but it can't hurt to ask. "Willie, I need to talk to Joseph Russo, Jr."

"Little Joey?" Willie asks, using a strange name for a mob leader.

"Right. Little Joey. You know him?"

"Sure. He's a good kid."

"He's into drugs, prostitution, and occasional murder."

"I've never seen any of that." For a guy who spent seven years locked up with the worst elements of our society, Willie is bliss-fully naïve and trusting.

"You might be right. Can you get me a meeting with him?"

"Sure. What should I tell him it's about?"

"Can you not give him a heads-up? I sort of want to surprise him."

"Sure. No problem."

There is literally nothing I could ask Willie for that he wouldn't respond with "Sure . . . no problem." Remarkably, he's usually right. We leave it that he will call Russo and try to set something up.

I head home to take Tara and Sebastian for their walk. Laurie has just dropped off Ricky at Will Rubenstein's for a sleepover, so she's free to walk with us.

I like taking walks with Laurie, but only when Sebastian is with us. Left to her own devices, Laurie is a fast walker. She treats it as exercise, and keeping up with her makes me feel like I'm on the Bataan Death March. Sebastian is my antidote to that; he lumbers along at such a slow pace that even I have no trouble keeping up. When it comes to going from point A to point B, I've seen sofa beds move faster than Sebastian.

I have no desire to think about the case, but Laurie brings it up. "I've been thinking. An important fact to consider is that whoever did this was not trying to frame Vogel; they were trying to kill him."

"What about the traces of explosives in his house?"

"We think that was done after the fact. He was already in custody, so the bad guys latched on to that as the second-best outcome. But first and foremost, they wanted him dead."

"What's your point?" I ask, though I see it. I want to make sure nothing is on her mind that I'm missing.

"It's likely that the reason they wanted to kill him still exists, especially if what they're afraid of is something that he knows. They could make another run at him."

"I should have thought of that. I'll put in a request for extra protection at the jail."

"Maybe I should be the one to do that." She says that because I am widely disliked by all levels of law enforcement, even more so than most defense attorneys.

"Are you implying that my charm might not be fully appreciated by some members of the jail staff?"

"That's one way of putting it; I was afraid I was being too subtle. A more direct way might be to say that your asking for

Vogel to be protected might actually prompt one of the guards to kill him."

"Then maybe you should make the request."

She nods. "Good idea. Did you tell Willie when you want to meet with Russo?"

"No. Whenever he sets it up will be okay. Willie is a trusting soul; he thinks Russo is a fine, upstanding gentleman."

"Right. A prince among men. I'm going to call around and see what we can find out about him; the more information you have going in the better."

Laurie means that she will contact some of her old friends on the police force whose job it is to put Russo and people like him behind bars. As research projects go, it's not exactly an unbiased sampling, but it could be helpful.

"Good idea. Find out if he's likely to be dazzled by my boyish charm."

"How can he not be? I know I am."

Willie obviously had no trouble arranging a meeting with Joseph Russo, Jr.

The meeting is tonight at eight o'clock at Russo's house in the Riverside section of Paterson. I know the area well; I used to watch professional softball games nearby at Riverside Oval with my father. Not only did I enjoy both the games and spending time with my father, but a vendor there sold the best Italian ice in the history of the world.

As promised, Laurie has contacted friends in the police department who could be considered experts on Russo. "So here's what I learned. Junior is said to be trying to bring the operation into the twentieth century."

"This is the twenty-first century," I point out.

"One step at a time. His father ran it with a Wild West mentality. Junior is trying to install a business model, even though he does not have a business background. His primary problem is lack of funds; his secondary problem is lack of smarts."

"I'm surprised to hear that. Prostitution, gambling, and drugs aren't moneymakers anymore?"

"They are, but there are still huge expenses. Russo's employees feel they should be well paid for committing crimes, and he seems to be having some trouble meeting that payroll.

Nothing he can't handle right now, but it could grow into a serious problem. He could start losing people, and when you're hiring professional killers, the prospective employee pool is not that large."

"Good to know."

"I think you should bring Marcus with you," Laurie says, as always scornful of my ability to handle myself.

"It won't be necessary; Willie will be there. It's an honor thing; Russo owes Willie for saving his father. He wouldn't do anything to me."

"What if this gangster murderer is not quite as honorable as you think?"

"I'll tell you what. Have Marcus in the area. If I need him, I'll press a button on my phone that will be set to text him. He can then do the Marcus version of a home invasion."

"Okay," she says reluctantly. "By the way, what are you hoping to accomplish with this?"

"I'm checking off a box, that's all. Vogel thinks Russo is behind it, and I'm doing my due diligence by following it up."

"How will meeting with him give you the answer? You're going to ask him if he did it and hope that he tells you the truth?"

"I'm just trying to assess his reaction. It's a technique we lawyers use; I call it reaction assessment."

"Clever name. I'll be calling Marcus."

Laurie tells me that she spoke to the authorities at the jail, and they promised to pay extra attention to making sure Vogel is safe. "They don't have solitary confinement down there, but they'll move him into a cell by himself, decrease his interaction with the other inmates, and increase their monitoring."

"Good job. Who did you speak to?"

"Roger Cousins."

I know Cousins; he's head of jail security, and therefore something less than a fan of mine. "Did you mention my name?"

"No, once he asked if I was still married to that 'asshole,' it didn't seem like a good idea."

"That Roger; he's some kidder."

Laurie, Ricky, and I have dinner; she makes penne Bolognese, which is Ricky's absolute favorite food. I like it as well, and I never take for granted that I am blessed to have a child that doesn't like vegetables.

Once we're done, I take Tara for a walk, then head to the Foundation. Willie and I will leave from there for the meeting with Russo, and this will give me a chance to spend some time with the rescue dogs and pretend I am doing my share.

Sondra brings Aggie down there each day as well; she loves to play with the other dogs. This gives me a chance to actually spend a little time with Aggie, so that when I tell Vogel that she's doing well, I can know what I'm talking about.

"She's doing great, Andy. She loves Cash, and he is nuts about her. He follows her everywhere." Cash is Willie and Sondra's dog; he and I found him running stray the day Willie collected a huge check for his wrongful-arrest suit. "If Vogel doesn't want her back, she's welcome in our family forever."

"I'm sure if he can take her back, he will," I say. "But in the meantime, I'm glad she's doing so well." She does seem happy, which is more than I can say for her owner's lawyer.

I won't say that I'm dreading the meeting with Russo, but it's close. I believe that Willie's presence will make me safe, at least for the length of the meeting, but I don't relish hanging out with members of organized crime. Knowing that the person I am talking to has had people killed is somehow unsettling.

Willie seems unconcerned, though as a general rule he is

impervious to concern. Laurie calls me to say that Marcus will be in place and ready to intervene if necessary, though he shares my belief that it won't come to that.

At seven thirty Willie says, "Let's go see Joey."

I nod. "Good old Joey."

Russo junior lives next door to where his father lived.

I'd been there once; I don't remember the details of why I was there, but I've got a feeling it wasn't for a frat party. I do remember that Willie was with me then, and I'm glad he's with me now.

By the time we get into the den to see Russo, we've been checked out by four bodyguards, who collectively must weigh at least fourteen hundred pounds. Two of the uglier ones frisk me, a distinctly unpleasant experience.

I've never met Russo nor seen a photo of him, so his appearance comes as something of a surprise. His father was, to coin a phrase, a fat slob. Very, very fat and very slobby. From behind he looked like a disheveled, jiggly refrigerator freezer.

Junior is the opposite; he looks to be in terrific shape. He's also dressed neatly in a sport shirt and khakis; his father considered himself overdressed in a sweatshirt.

Laurie's cop friends had said that Junior is trying to convey a more businesslike approach, and that seems consistent with his appearance and demeanor.

He's sitting at a desk when we walk in. When he sees Willie, Russo grins broadly and the two men hug. "Willie, my man."

Willie responds with "Joey."

"How goes it? You need anything?"

"Nah. Going good."

These two guys can really keep a conversation going; I feel like I'm witness to a rebirth of the Algonquin Round Table.

Russo and Willie break off the hug, prompting Russo to look at me for the first time. His apparent pleasure at seeing Willie evaporates. "You're Carpenter."

"That's uncanny," I say.

"I hear from everybody that you're an asshole."

"It's just nice to know people are talking about me."

"Andy's okay," Willie says, a welcome intervention.

Russo thinks for a moment, then nods. "If Willie says you're okay, maybe you're okay. Of course, even Willie isn't right one hundred percent of the time. What do you want?"

"Do you know Alex Vogel?"

Russo stiffens instantly. "No," he says, clearly lying through his teeth. Based on his reaction, he absolutely either knows Vogel or knows about him.

"Are you sure?" It's basically a meaningless question. I've already learned what little I'm going to learn from this meeting.

Russo turns to Willie. "Your okay friend doesn't understand what no means."

I had planned not to mention Russo's now-deceased girlfriend, nor her connection to Vogel. I figured on the off chance that Russo didn't know about their relationship, I shouldn't be the one to break the news. Vogel has enough problems without enlisting Russo as an enemy.

"He's my client. He's the man accused of blowing up that boat with two people on it. Maybe you read about it."

"I didn't."

"Okay. I know you're an influential guy in the community,

and that you hear things. So I thought maybe you heard something about him."

"Is that right? You know what I heard? I heard maybe it's healthier for him to be in jail. That's what I heard."

"Would you care to elaborate on that?"

Russo turns to Willie, apparently having tired of me. "Willie, you're welcome here anytime. You were my father's man, so you're my man. But I think you should get your friend out of here."

Willie nods. "Yeah. Be good, Joey."

"Stay cool, Will."

Willie and I leave. I text Marcus the news that we have left and don't need his help. I'm glad we didn't, though it would have been a treat to watch him manhandle Russo's four bodyguards.

Willie and I don't talk about the meeting on the way to his house, except for my thanking him for setting it up.

"Anytime" is his response.

I drop him off and head home to tell Laurie what transpired. She hugs me hello, an unspoken admission that she was at least a little worried about me.

We sit in the den with a glass of wine while I tell her my impressions of the meeting. "He definitely knew Vogel, even though he denied it. He clearly reacted when he heard his name, and his demeanor completely changed."

"Changed how?"

"He got angry, and then even after telling me twice that he didn't know Vogel and never heard of him, he basically threatened him. He said he was safer in jail than he would be on the outside."

"So is he a suspect now?"

"Let's just say he's not eliminated. I still don't see him sending hit men out on the ocean to a yacht, but I don't have anyone better."

She nods. "Okay, so yesterday we had no suspects, and today we sort of have one. That's progress."

"Moving right along."

Hike had visited with Vogel and gotten a rundown on his life.

Other than the ill-fated relationship with Joseph Russo's girlfriend, not much seemed like a promising lead or theory. Laurie and Corey Douglas have been going through it all and interviewing people mentioned, but have not reported anything worth pursuing further.

Vogel has lived a rather uneventful life, dominated by work. He got married right out of college, but it only lasted two years. His ex-wife has remarried, moved to Seattle, and has three kids with her new husband. She and Vogel are no longer in touch, and he said the breakup was relatively amicable. It seems somewhat unlikely that all these years later she would hire two men to blow up her ex-husband on his boat.

He didn't have that many friends. A group of six guys occasionally played poker and went to Knicks games, but Laurie said nothing casts any suspicion on any of them.

Dating Carla D'Antoni was something of an aberration for Vogel. With that notable exception, his dating life resembled my high school romantic exploits, which is to say they were basically nonexistent.

Laurie is trying to get updated on the investigation into

D'Antoni's death from friends on the police force. Once she does, we'll delve into her life a bit and see if we can learn anything relevant to our case.

I still don't believe that her relationship with Vogel caused Russo to send his men out on a high-seas mission to murder three people; it seems like literal overkill. But one never knows.

Vogel, by his own telling, does not seem the type to have taken up with D'Antoni. I am not saying that the circumstances seem suspicious, nor do I have any reason why they might be. But I'm reserving judgment until I find out more about it.

I don't think the D'Antoni angle is particularly promising, but we're not exactly inundated with positive leads. We just have to keep checking investigative boxes until we hit pay dirt. Or not.

I wake up at seven, which is typical for me. I hear the whirring noise of Laurie on her exercise bike, which is also no surprise. She doesn't seem put off that she can ride for an hour and not get anywhere.

She always has a look of pure joy on her face when she finishes. I guess she and I have that in common. If I was crazy enough to exhaust myself by pedaling furiously to nowhere, I would also be happy when it was over.

I get ready to walk Ricky to school, until Laurie reminds me that it's Memorial Day. I had no idea; when I work on a case, I get so caught up in it that I tune out everything else. Unless it's football season; I never tune out football.

Instead I take Ricky down to the Tara Foundation. He loves to go there and play with the dogs. We always have twenty-five available for adoption, and Ricky pets every one of them. His personal favorite at the moment is a large black Lab named Bruiser. I don't blame him; two dogs is enough for our house, but if we were going to add a third, Bruiser would be a great choice.

We've been here for about forty-five minutes when Laurie calls and tells me that Vogel called from the jail. He needs to see me on what he describes as an important matter.

I leave Ricky at the Foundation; Willie will drive him home when he's had his fill of playing with the dogs. Knowing Ricky, that could take a couple of months. I just hope Ricky doesn't talk Willie into letting him bring Bruiser home.

I head down to the jail. My hope is that Vogel has remembered something that can be helpful, something like the real killers' names, addresses, and motive. I'm actually not expecting much; if Vogel is a typical client, he's as likely to pump me for information as he is to provide any.

I'm brought into the lawyer visiting room, and the guard brings Vogel in five minutes later. I can see excitement on his face; either something good has happened or he's got information to give me that he clearly thinks will be helpful.

He doesn't waste any time. "I know who one of the killers is."

"Tell me."

"Well, I don't know his name, I couldn't hear the announcer real well, but . . ."

He's rushing his words and not making a lot of sense. "Slow down, Alex. Just tell me what you know; I'm not going anywhere."

He nods. "Okay. Sorry, I'm just really excited by this. They let the prisoners here watch an hour of television a day. Usually I'm not allowed; they seem to think I need some extra protection or something."

I don't interrupt to say that it's a result of Laurie's request; I want him to continue.

"But today they let me do it. The news was on and there was a story about two guys that were killed. Their bodies were left in a park or something. I think it happened a while ago; this was like an update on the investigation.

"Anyway, I didn't get the names, but they showed pictures of the two dead guys, and one of them was the killer I saw on the boat."

"Are you sure?"

"Close to positive. I really think it was him. The other guy might have been there as well, but I never saw his face."

"Good. I'll get right on it. I may have Hike come down here with more photos of them to confirm the identification."

"Hike?" Alex is clearly not relishing the prospect.

Since he's already spent time with Hike, I'm not surprised that he's not looking forward to a repeat of that experience. An hour with Hike feels like a month. A miserable month. "I believe I had mentioned that he's not a laugh-a-minute kind of guy."

"You were right about that."

"What did he say?"

"Well, I don't remember how we got on the subject, but he started telling me about the number of people who die in prison. He said the food was so unsanitary that I'd be better off eating dirt, and that New Jersey compensates for not having a death penalty by using prison food to kill the inmates."

"That does sound like Hike. But you should try and tune him out; he really is a good lawyer, and he's on our side."

"If you say so."

"While I'm here, tell me how you came to meet Carla D'Antoni."

"It was after work; me and some friends would occasionally go to a restaurant/bar near the office to have a drink. It's called the Windward. Do you know it?"

"No."

"Anyway, we're sitting at the bar . . . actually that night I was there with Stephen Mellman . . . and this woman comes in and sits not too far from me. There was no one between us."

"What did you do?"

"Nothing. The next woman I start a conversation with at a bar will be the first. Fear of rejection, you know? Anyway, she orders a drink and then smiles at me. So I smile back. Then she asked me something. I don't remember what it was, nothing important. Maybe, did I work around there, or something like that. A conversational icebreaker.

"The next thing I know we're chatting away, and then we get a table and have dinner. I was a good ten years older than her, and she was really attractive. I figured, probably nothing will happen, but why not give it a shot?"

"What happened to Mellman?"

"He told me to go for it and then disappeared. He was being a good friend. I think he was also a little amazed, like I was."

"Did you go anywhere afterwards?"

"Amazingly, yes. Back to my house. That was how all our dates ended, always at my house. She said her roommate was a pain in the ass."

He shakes his head. "If I had any idea what would happen . . ." He doesn't have to say any more; I can see it in his face. He is facing that he may be responsible for her death.

"You're not the reason she died."

"You can't know that. But do me a favor? Prove me wrong."

I leave and call Sam Willis as soon as I get in the car. "Sam, did you see the story about the murder victims in Pennington Park?"

"Are they part of our case?" He's clearly thrilled that we might be involved with something dangerous. Nothing like a couple of assassinations to brighten Sam's day.

"Very possibly. So I need to know everything you can dig up about them. You need their names?"

"Andy, come on, give me some credit."

"Okay. Please get back to me as soon as you can."

"I'm on it."

liked you better when you were retired," Pete Stanton says. "Maybe a better way to put it is that I disliked you less."

"What a beautiful thing to say. Have you got a tissue?" I'm in Pete's office looking for a favor. After what I did to him when he tried to question Alex Vogel, a favor might not be something he will be looking to grant.

"What the hell do you want?"

"Information. Two guys, Charlie Phillips and Orlando Bledsoe, were killed and their bodies left in Pennington Park."

"Really? How come I didn't know about this? Oh, wait a minute. I'm head of homicide, and those were homicides. So maybe I'm already working on it."

"Based on your history, working on it means getting nowhere and then filing it away. Nobody has created more unsolved cases than you; you were Man of the Year in *Cold Case* magazine."

"You trying to get on my good side? I'll ask one more time before I throw your ambulance-chasing ass out of here: What the hell do you want?"

"I want to get information on the case."

"You're getting ahead of yourself; we haven't arrested anybody yet. You can't defend a scumbag and start collecting your ridiculously high fee until we arrest said scumbag."

"Tell me about the two victims."

"Why?"

I knew he would ask that, and I've thought about it. I don't see any downside in telling him what we believe. If he uses it and comes up with exculpatory evidence for Vogel, I know he'll bring it forward. Pete, like any cop, likes to make arrests and convictions. But he likes the truth more.

"I have reason to believe that Orlando Bledsoe, and most likely both of them, were the guys who set off the explosives on the boat."

"Vogel's boat?"

"No, the *Lusitania.* Come on, Pete, try to keep up."

"So in your pathetic attempt to help your client escape justice, you're scouring the news reports for dead guys to blame?"

"Vogel saw Bledsoe on the boat."

Pete frowns. "Sure. And then Bledsoe said, 'I'm going to let you live, but you need to go into hiding for weeks.'"

"Pete, who are these guys?"

He looks like he's going to argue some more, but then sighs. "They're hired guns. Used to work for Petrone, then Russo senior. Once those two bosses both bit the dust, they went out on their own."

Dominic Petrone was head of the crime family, actually the founder, before he departed this world. Joseph Russo, Sr., took over, then also involuntarily moved on.

"Why did they leave?"

"Russo junior is said to be in a bit of a money crunch. He's reduced his staff."

"Could they have still been working for Junior on a contract basis?"

"Always possible. They'd work for whoever paid them."

"Who might have killed them?"

"Somebody very good and very dangerous."

"Do you know why?"

Pete shakes his head. "Not yet."

"Allow me to speculate. They were killed because they screwed up and failed to kill Alex Vogel."

"Allow me to speculate. You're full of shit."

"While we're talking about cases you can't come close to solving, how are you doing on Carla D'Antoni's murder?"

He smiles, though it's more of a smirk than a smile. "You know about that?"

"About what?"

"That your client was sleeping with her. Maybe you'll have another trial to make money on."

"What does that mean?"

"It means that a lot of people in Alex Vogel's world seem to turn up dead."

I laugh. "You think Vogel killed her?"

"You'll know that soon enough, Counselor."

"You going to make him for the Kennedy assassination also? He could have been in Dallas that day; I heard he's a Cowboys fan."

"Let's just say he'll get what he deserves."

"What's the record for most stupid mistakes by one cop on one case?"

"The only mistake I can think of was taking this meeting, which is now officially over."

Russo's name keeps turning up," I say.

   "First the D'Antoni connection, but now Bledsoe and Phillips." I'm talking and drinking wine with Laurie in the den. Ricky has been asleep for a couple of hours, and Tara and Sebastian have been walked.

So let the murder talk begin.

"But you still don't think he's involved?" Laurie asks.

I shake my head. "No. I can't get past the fact that it was done out on the ocean. It's just not his style. Also, if it was Russo, he wouldn't have framed Vogel by leaving explosive traces in his house when he failed to kill him. Russo would just have tried to kill him again."

"Bledsoe and Phillips got a single bullet in the head. That would be very much Russo's style."

I can't argue with that, so I don't make the attempt. "It could be that I'm reading too much into it. Pete says that the two of them broke away from Russo and went on their own. He had no evidence that they were still working for him.

"And so what if there once was a connection? They're criminals and he's the head of an organized crime family. Of course they crossed paths; they're part of the same business. Maybe they spoke on the same panels at crime conventions. I know plenty of lawyers, don't I?"

"But it's still a coincidence," Laurie says. "And the last time I checked, we don't believe in coincidences."

"No, we don't. But in one way it almost doesn't matter."

"What do you mean?"

"Trell will have no trouble placing Vogel on that boat, and even less trouble getting the jury to understand that he acted guilty by hiding and letting everyone think he was dead."

"So?"

"So my only shot with the jury is going to be to point to another potential killer. And that person has to be credible. When it comes to potential killers, Russo is as credible as they get. So whether I really believe it or not, I am going to have to introduce evidence about Russo and make the jury think he could have ordered it. That gives me at least a chance at reasonable doubt."

"They're still going to want an explanation for why Vogel acted the way he did."

"He was afraid of Russo because of the affair with D'Antoni. It's not the greatest story I've ever heard, but Vogel says it's true, and from his point of view it makes sense. She was killed and then somebody tried to kill him, so he connected it to Russo."

"So you'll put Vogel on the stand to tell that story?" She's clearly surprised at the possibility.

"It's the nightmare scenario, but I might have to. There's no one else to tell it." Defense attorneys generally loathe putting defendants on the stand and subjecting them to cross-examination. "The problem is that Trell will have him for lunch."

"This trial will get a lot of media attention," Laurie says. "There's a pretty good chance that Russo will not appreciate your calling him a murderer."

"What about if I smile when I say it?"

"You do have an adorable smile."

I nod. "And that certainly should be enough, but just in case there are one or two members of the jury resistant to my charms, I could use some corroboration. Pete knew that D'Antoni was dating Vogel. He had to have heard it from someone."

"D'Antoni had a sister. I was about to tell you about her."

"Have you contacted her?"

Laurie nods. "I have."

"Would she talk to me?"

"She'd like nothing better."

"Because of my smile?"

"No doubt about it." Then, "Let's go to bed."

I silently ask myself, *Did she just say what I think she said?* I don't mean the words; I heard them clearly. It's the meaning I am unclear on, and in matters of this type, clarity is important to me. "You mean bed-bed? Or just bed?"

She shakes her head and smiles. "I married a fourteen-year-old."

"I'm just trying to understand the situation; it will determine whether I brush my teeth."

"Brush them. I mean bed-bed."

I am trying to stifle a stupid grin when the phone rings. It's unusually late for us to be getting a call, so Laurie stays downstairs and waits to hear who it is as I answer it.

It's Sam Willis. "Andy, I'm ready to give you a partial report on the two dead guys in Pennington Park. Can I come over? I can be there in ten minutes."

"Come over? Now?" I'm horrified at the prospect. I don't add that I am preparing for bed-bed.

"I've got some important stuff to tell you."

"Will it still be important in the morning?"

"Of course."

"Then let's do it then. My mind will be fresher and more absorbent."

"Okay. Whatever you say."

"That's what I say. Thanks."

I hang up the phone and turn to Laurie. "Wrong number."

There's a lot still out there for me to learn," Sam says.

If I needed further reassurance that I was right in opting for bed-bed rather than a late-night meeting with Sam, and I don't, then this opening statement has provided it.

"I found an interesting thread, so I just kept pulling on it. You know what I mean?"

"Yes, Sam. We understand the thread-pulling analogy." I look over at Laurie, sitting at the kitchen table with us. She avoids rolling her eyes, quite a feat in these circumstances. Mine have already done three complete circles.

"I figured you did. I got the cell phone numbers for Phillips and Bledsoe and did a deep dive on them. Tracked calls in and out, GPS information, everything."

Sam has the ability to get into the phone company computers and unlock the amazing amount of information that cell phone use can yield. It's not legal for him to do it, but I've come to terms with that. I'm sure the police have already done it for these phones as part of their own investigation, so I see Sam's work as evening the playing field.

We can't get this kind of information in discovery because we can't yet make a showing that Phillips and Bledsoe have anything to do with our case. Therefore the cops, and prosecution, have no reason to provide it to us.

Which brings us to Sam.

"There was nothing significant to be found," Sam says. "The phones were rarely used or taken anywhere. Calls and texts, which were few and far between, were a waste of time."

"Sounds promising." For some reason Sam's style is to reveal negative news first and relate everything so slowly it makes me want to grab and shake him. "Can we move this along? Maybe get to the good stuff?"

"Sure. Anyway, I figured that nobody uses phones like that; I mean, everyone lives on their phones, right? So I checked their credit-card records, and Bledsoe had made a purchase for seventy bucks at an electronics store in Paramus. On a hunch, I went into the store computer. And bingo."

"Bingo?"

Sam nods. "Double bingo. He bought two burner phones."

I can see Laurie sit up a little straighter when she hears this; it could well be leading to news that is worthy of a double bingo.

"There were a bunch of calls on them, especially on Bledsoe's phone, but I haven't gotten names and addresses to attach to them yet. I will."

"How do you know which phone was Bledsoe's?"

"That's the good news. Some burners don't have GPS systems in them, but these phones were top-of-the-line, so they did. I could see which phone spent time at Bledsoe's address, and which one was at Phillips's house. Piece of cake."

"So tell us the good news," Laurie says.

Sam nods. "Here it comes. On the day that the boat explosion happened, both phones were down in Toms River. So I did some more checking; Bledsoe chartered a boat. He used a credit card."

"Triple bingo," Laurie says.

"Sam, get out of here and get back to work. If you come up with more stuff like this, we'll let you shoot somebody."

"Don't tease me," he says, but leaves to illegally invade more computers.

Once he's gone, Laurie says, "This is huge."

"It can be, if I can figure out how to use it."

She shakes her head. "You're thinking like a lawyer."

"What a terrible thing to say."

She laughs. "No, I mean it. For now, forget how you will get it in front of a jury; instead pull back and look at the big picture. This proves that Vogel is telling the truth about what happened. If Bledsoe and Phillips chartered a boat twenty miles away that day, then they killed those people. They had to; there cannot be a coincidence that big."

Laurie is absolutely right. I had never fully believed Vogel's story, but it has essentially now been completely corroborated.

"Which means that our goal is at least capable of being accomplished," I say. "Before we were trying to prove something that might not be true. At least now we know it is."

"Exactly."

"And it gives me another chance to look past the positive and focus on the negative."

"You find a negative in this?" she asks. "Why am I asking? Of course you do."

"Look, I'm obviously glad he's innocent, and also glad that we have an opportunity to uncover real facts. That outweighs everything else."

"But . . ."

"But it ratchets up the pressure exponentially. Now if I lose, there is no doubt that an innocent man will spend the rest of his life in prison. Before it was at least conceivable that a loss would mean a murderer would get the punishment he deserves."

"I have the solution to that," she says.

"And that is?"

"Let's win."

Ricky's leaving for camp today.

The way it works is that we, and all the other parents, drive our kids to a designated place in Ridgewood, where they all board the bus to camp. I dread the process; I can't stand that I won't see him for weeks.

Dread is not how I would describe Ricky's attitude; he loved camp so much last year that he's been waiting for this day to come for months. Any pain that he might feel in missing his father has not revealed itself yet.

Laurie shipped his clothing to the camp, per their direction. This year each camper is only allowed one large trunk, which was a problem because she had bought enough to fill two large tractor trailers.

So Laurie had to decide which clothes to ship and which to leave behind, a task she took seriously. She developed a strategy and implemented it; it took a great deal of time and planning.

Think D-Day, only with boys' underwear.

The bus pulls up and it's time to say good-bye. Laurie and I each hug Ricky, wish him a great summer, and tell him how much we will miss him. Laurie cries openly and I pretend not to be affected.

It's a lie; I am totally and completely affected. I am going to miss the hell out of him. But I know he is going to have a great time, so I think I'll hold on to that.

It annoys me that the parents cheer when the bus pulls away, but Laurie and I don't linger to chat with any of them. I'm going to drop her off at home and then go see Robby Divine.

I'm wealthy, the result of an inheritance and some lucrative cases. But Robby Divine is in another class; he's thirty-four years old and *Forbes* says he is worth $16 billion. He was pissed when the magazine came out, claiming that they undervalued some assets. Money is the way he keeps score.

I figured out once that in thirty-four years he had lived a little over one billion seconds, but he managed in that time to accumulate $16 billion. I'm not sure why I bothered to figure that out.

Robby told me once that if you converted all his money into hundred-dollar bills and laid them end to end, you'd never finish because he keeps making so much money.

Robby is slightly obsessed with money.

We met about five years ago at an insufferable charity dinner; one of those occasions where I would much rather have not gone and instead written a check. I would have thrown in the cost of my surf-and-turf dinner.

Robby and I were the only people there not wearing ties but wearing sneakers. We became sort of friends, and he's the guy I turn to when I need information about the world of high finance. I'm the guy he turns to . . . never.

He lives in the city but plays golf at a country-club course in Alpine, New Jersey. I head there to meet him in the clubhouse, where he's waiting for me after playing eighteen holes. He introduces me to three of his friends, then we go off to a table to have a drink and talk.

"What does my peasant friend want to discuss today?" he asks. "Since baseball is off the table at the moment."

Robby is a fanatic Chicago Cubs fan. They lost yesterday, which is why he is not wearing his Cubs cap right now. He gets extremely bitter after a loss, as if they have let him down personally. Baseball will cease to exist for him again until they win a game.

"Pharmacon," I say.

"As long as we're going to talk about pathetic losers, we might as well talk about the Cubs."

"Pharmacon is a pathetic loser?"

"I may have overstated it. What do you want to know?"

"I'm not sure."

He nods. "That's my favorite thing about you, your clarity of thought."

"It's one of my best features, second only to my smile. Can you just talk about them, tell me what you know?"

He frowns, but complies. "They're one of ten million pharmaceutical start-ups. As we're talking, some of them are going under. It's a capital-intensive business, heavily regulated, which makes it harder on them."

"Harder how?"

"Harder How? Who does he pitch for?" Then, "The process of going through the various testing protocols and ultimately getting FDA approval for a drug is time-consuming, and time is money. It's a hit-or-miss business, and the bankruptcy courts are filled with misses. That's why the big companies dominate the field: they can afford the misses."

"But it can be lucrative?"

"Absolutely; if one hits, the profit can be enormous."

"Pharmacon is doing an IPO."

He frowns his disdain. "Not going to do well; they would

be better off not going forward, but they need the money. It's a tough situation because they would do much better if they had positive news to tell."

"Are you buying any shares?"

"I looked at it, but I'm not interested. They're pricing it at ten dollars a share, and it sold out, but it will go down from there."

"How did it sell out if it's not a good buy?"

"Must be a lot of buying within the company and by hand-picked investors. I don't have any personal knowledge of this, but some of the money might not be squeaky-clean."

If I had antennae, they would have just gone way up. "What do you mean?"

"It's a way to launder money. You buy stock through a shell company, hold it for a little while, sell it, and you've run it through the washing machine. As long as the company you're buying into is willing to not look too closely, then it doesn't matter that much if the stock goes up or down. The point is not to make a profit, it's to launder the money.

"Like I say, I have no idea whether that happened, but by the time I looked at it, there was nothing left, although I wouldn't have bought in anyway." Then, "Hey, those were Pharmacon guys who died on that boat. Is that why you're interested in this?"

"Guilty as charged."

"Good. I was afraid you were investing in their IPO. I don't want you to become one of those friends I have to loan money to."

"Do you know the top guy there? Eric Buckner? I met with him."

Robby shakes his head. "I've met him, but I don't know much about him. He's a science guy who thinks he knows finance. You can count the number of science guys who really understand money on very few fingers."

"Bill Gates."

"He's one of the fingers."

"Buckner said I could talk to whoever I wanted in the company."

"Then go see the CFO, Gerald Bennings. He knows what he's talking about, at least compared to Buckner."

I thank Robby and leave, a little disappointed. I was hoping that huge money was to be made at Pharmacon. Vogel and the two victims worked there, and it is not rare to find murders connected in some fashion to the chance to get rich.

Robby has seemed to dampen that possibility, if not killing it entirely. I would have been better off talking about the Cubs.

I t was like watching a slow-motion train wreck." Linda D'Antoni is talking about her late sister, Carla. "But there was no way to stop it from happening. It's the worst, most frustrating thing I've ever experienced, and nothing is in second place."

We're talking in the downstairs cafeteria in Hackensack Hospital, where Linda works as an intensive-care nurse. She's just finished her shift and looks exhausted, but is obviously anxious to talk about her sister.

"Tell me about her." I want to hear the general before I ask the specific; I find I learn more that way.

"That's not the easiest thing to do. There were two Carlas; she was one person and then she was another. Looking back, I still can't believe it."

Linda shakes her head in sadness at the memory. "We lived together in a house in Leonia when we moved here, close to five years ago. Then, all of a sudden, she moved out. Said it had nothing to do with me; she just wanted to live on her own. She said she needed her space. So she rented a studio apartment in Lyndhurst. Can you imagine? She took a studio apartment because she needed space. I still don't know what was going on with her."

"Maybe a boyfriend?"

"No maybe about it, but it was more than one. She started going out a lot, hanging out with people she never would have hung out with before. I guess there was a quality about Carla that enjoyed some danger, living on the edge a bit, but she always kept that under control. That changed."

"Did she talk about her boyfriends?"

"Why do you want to know all this stuff?"

It took her longer to ask the question than I had expected. "I have a client who is accused of murder. I think the people that actually committed the murder may have been Carla's killers as well. I'm just trying to put together as much information as I can."

Linda considers this for a few moments. "Okay. Maybe you can get somewhere. The police don't seem to be making any progress. She mentioned a few boyfriends in passing, mostly just first names."

"Any you can remember?"

"Chuck . . . Danny . . . Joseph . . . Rick . . . she mentioned Rick a few times. I can't think of any others."

"Alex?"

"No, I don't think so."

"Did she say Joseph's last name?"

"You mean because of that media story about Joseph Russo? I read about that in the paper, but Carla never mentioned any last name. There's one other thing. . . ."

"What's that?"

"In those last couple of months, Carla all of a sudden had money. I don't know where she got it from, but she was buying things, picking up checks. I never asked her how; I think I was afraid to."

"Do you know where she got the money?"

"No, but she wasn't hiding it. She even told me she would

give me stock tips." Linda shakes her head sadly again; I have a feeling she does that a lot these days. "She never got to do that, or a lot of other things."

"Where did she work?"

"She was a hairstylist, a really good one. But that's not where she got her money. When she died, I called the salon to make sure they knew what happened, and they told me she hadn't been there for three weeks. Never called and told them why and never told me anything about it."

"Where are her things?"

"At my place. I packed up her apartment, but haven't gone through them yet. I'm working up the nerve."

"If you find anything that might relate to what was happening in her life, I would appreciate your telling me. You should tell the police is well."

Linda takes a deep breath, as if girding herself for the ordeal of going through her sister's things. "I will. I should have done it already. And if you learn anything about what happened to her, will you tell me?"

"I will."

She stands to leave, but then stops. "She was my little sister and no matter what, my best friend. I still can't quite wrap my head around the fact that she's gone."

There's nothing that I can say that will make Linda feel better, so I don't try.

She has told me a few interesting things. One is that Carla was dating fairly indiscriminately. Vogel seemed to think they had a more significant relationship, and he was apparently wrong about that. She also didn't have a particularly special connection to Russo either, if Linda's comments are to be taken at face value.

Much more interesting is Carla's apparently coming into

some money not long before she died. This case might ultimately come down to money, so if someone was giving a bunch of it to Carla, then that person would be of interest to me.

There could be a benign explanation for it. Maybe one of her boyfriends just gave her money because he liked her or was showing off. So what? It happens all the time and is rarely sinister.

One thing is curious, at least to me. While Linda said that Carla never mentioned Alex Vogel, Pete Stanton knew about the relationship. He even made a veiled threat to charge Vogel with Carla's murder. Clearly he didn't hear about it from Linda, so I would like to know who his source was. It might be significant. Or not.

The bottom line is that I've gotten some insight into Carla from Linda, maybe even a lot, but not nearly enough.

There's one way to rectify that, and I should have done it a while ago. I call Sam and tell him to get on checking out Carla D'Antoni.

"Okay, good timing. I'm just wrapping up the work on Phillips and Bledsoe's burner phones. As soon as I'm finished, I'll start on this."

"There's a bunch of pancakes in it for you if you come up with something good."

had called to try to set up a meeting with Gerald Bennings. He's the CFO at Pharmacon, and Robby said he was the guy I should talk to there. Robby seemed to imply that Bennings was not a complete idiot, which represents a ringing endorsement coming from Robby.

I mentioned Robby's name when I called, and I suggested that Bennings could check about me with his boss, Eric Buckner. After all, Buckner had said he would give his okay for his employees to meet with me.

Checking with Buckner turned out not to be necessary for Bennings; that I knew Robby was enough to get me in the door. And that is where I am now . . . in the door. More specifically, I am in Bennings's office at Pharmacon.

"I'm surprised Robby suggested you talk to me," Bennings says. "I assumed he was pissed at me."

"Maybe he is and saw talking to me as getting his revenge. But why would he be pissed at you?"

"Because he couldn't get in on the IPO; he looked at it too late."

Robby told me he had no interest in buying into Pharmacon, and Bennings is implying otherwise. I don't care who is telling the truth, but I suspect it's Robby.

"He told me he thinks you should wait to go public, that you're pricing too low."

Bennings smiles. "Robby lives in a world where having enough capital is not a problem. If he were sitting behind this desk, and if he didn't personally have a basket full of billions, he might view things differently."

"When is the IPO?"

"I actually can't talk about it. We're in the quiet period."

I have no idea what a quiet period is, but I think I'll try to use one on Hike. "What can you tell me about Alex Vogel, Stephen Mellman, and Robert Giarrusso?"

"Salt of the earth, all three of them. They did their jobs, did them well, and always had a good attitude. It's horrible what happened, but the police have it wrong. There is no way Alex Vogel should be in jail."

That's exactly what his boss, Buckner, said. I wish I could get them on the jury. "Stephen Mellman worked for you?"

Bennings nods. "Yes, so I definitely knew him better than Alex and Robert. None of them will be easy to replace."

"Would Mellman have been involved in setting up the IPO?"

"In the very early stages, but most of the work was done after he died."

"Buckner told me he assumes the three of them were planning to leave and start their own company."

Bennings shrugs. "Certainly could be. Happens every day."

"Any idea why they would do that? Did they think things were not promising here?"

"I have no idea what they thought about our prospects. Most likely Giarrusso was working on a new drug idea that the three of them thought they could capitalize on. With Vogel in research, Giarrusso handing the science, and Mellman raising the money, they would have thought they had all their bases covered."

"Could it have worked?"

"Depending on the drug, and depending on how much money they could raise, which would in turn depend on the drug." Then, "It's not an easy business, but everyone wants to take their shot."

"Can you think of any reason anyone in your world might have thought of them, or Alex Vogel in particular, as enemies?"

Bennings considers the possibility for a few moments, then shakes his head. "I'm sorry, no."

"Do the names Charlie Phillips and Orlando Bledsoe mean anything to you?"

Another shake of the head. "No. Who are they?"

"It's who 'were' they. They're both murder victims."

He half recoils. "And are they also involved in this case?"

"Could be. Welcome to my world."

"And I thought this was a tough business. I'll ask around, but I never heard of them."

"Thanks. Good luck."

"You mean with the IPO?"

I put my fingers to my lips. "Shhh . . . quiet period."

I t was a typical morning for Jeremy Bowers, and that was the problem.

Every day was almost identical to the one before, and the one before that, going back the eight years since Bowers had arrived at Strickland Laboratories in Monticello, New York.

He had received a number of promotions, culminating in his ascension to lab director three and a half years ago. But basically the job had not changed; there were no ups or downs, no new challenges.

Bowers had kept up with the changes that technology had brought, and he rightfully believed that Strickland Labs was as modern and competent as anything the big cities had to offer. But that didn't help with daily drudgery.

Bowers just showed up, did his job, and did it well.

Day after day after day.

That is why every free moment he had was spent in the wood-working shop he built for himself at home. That was his true love, and his hope and expectation was that in the not-too-distant future it would become his occupation. He would open a store and sell the furniture that he made.

But until then he did his job conscientiously, as rote as it was. Even lunch hour was the same. He always ate with his second-in-command, Allen Julian, in the building cafeteria. Strickland Labs shared it with an accounting firm; each company occupied half of the six-story building.

Julian had arrived at the company three years earlier and quickly rose to the number two position. He was clearly Bowers's chosen successor, though nothing indicated that the transfer would take place anytime soon.

The two men rarely talked about work during lunch; discussing bacteria cultures was just not that interesting. So they talked sports or politics or whatever else came up as the subject of the day. Mostly sports; Bowers was a Yankee fan, and Julian preferred the Mets, so Bowers usually had the upper hand when it came to competitive comparisons.

Despite the time they spent together at lunches, Bowers knew little about Julian. He knew Julian was competent at his job and more familiar with modern techniques than Bowers himself.

But he had no idea the extent of Julian's ambition and how he had long been angling to remove Bowers and take over his position. Bowers was also completely unaware that Julian was having an affair with Bowers's wife. These are the kinds of things that Julian understandably did not raise at lunch.

They had a routine; since it was cafeteria-style, one of them would go on the food line and get the meals for both of them. The other would get the drinks, and they'd meet at their regular table.

Today, Bowers got the food and Julian took care of the drinks. They then ate in relative silence; what talking they did was about baseball and what the New York teams might do at the trade deadline.

After lunch they went back to their respective offices. Julian could then do nothing but wait for what he knew was about to happen.

Somewhere around three o'clock, he would get a call from a panicked coworker that Bowers had collapsed. Julian would rush over and watch the medical personnel frantically and unsuccessfully try to resuscitate his fallen boss.

An ambulance would take Bowers away, and he would be pronounced dead either on the way to the hospital or soon after arrival there. The initial suspicion would be that he had had a massive coronary, and an autopsy would subsequently confirm it. The death would be considered due to natural causes; certainly there was no reason to suspect foul play.

Everything went exactly as Julian knew that it would, with one minor exception.

The call came at three fifteen.

Carla D'Antoni led a pretty active social life," Sam says. This just confirms what her sister told me, but I ask, "How so?"

"There were a lot of text messages on her phone to different guys, and she slept at a number of different places over the course of the last few months. Or let's say that her phone did."

This is already making me a little uncomfortable. Carla is dead, brutally murdered, and it feels wrong to be invading her privacy like this. Unfortunately, I have to do it if I am going to fully defend my client.

We're in my office; one of my rare times here. It's just easier to work from home, especially with Laurie there. But I needed Edna here to type some motions that Hike will present to the court. So she and Hike are in Hike's office. Between her dismay at having to work, and Hike's ability to depress and annoy, chances are decent that she will be the only one to come out of that office alive.

"Was Vogel's house one of the places she stayed over?"

Sam nods. "Seven times."

"What about Russo?"

"Nope."

That surprises me; maybe the reports of her being Russo's

girlfriend were wrong. But Russo is not the type to have met Carla at a hotel. He would be concerned about his personal safety, so would always want the home-field advantage. Yet Russo reacted when I mentioned Vogel's name, so I just assumed there was some rivalry there over Carla.

"Let me check that to make sure." Sam goes down the hall to get his notes. He's back within three minutes with a briefcase full of folders, and he takes one out and starts going through it.

"No, I don't see Russo's house anywhere. Maybe she met him somewhere else."

"Okay."

He continues to look through the papers, then finally says, "Wait a minute."

"What is it?"

"Something looks familiar. . . ." He opens the briefcase again and takes out two more folders. He starts poring through them. I'm not going to get anywhere by asking him what is going on; it would just slow him down.

"Wow," he finally says.

"What are you wowing about, Sam?"

"Based on her phone GPS, she was at an address on Market Street in Paterson from seven forty-five until nine thirty. It turns out it was a bar called Masters." He looks at the papers in front of him again. "That was a week before she died."

"So?"

"So it hit me that the address seemed familiar, and now I know why. Bledsoe went to that place all the time, maybe five times a week. Phillips was there as well, but not as often."

"Were they there the same night?"

"Good question." Sam turns back to his papers and within fifteen seconds says, "They were. Bledsoe got there twenty minutes before her and stayed an hour afterwards. Phillips was there as well, but he got there after Carla left."

"Wow" was the appropriate comment for Sam to make; this is a major development. If Carla knew and met with Bledsoe, and if Bledsoe blew up Vogel's boat, then it completely changes my view of Carla, as it relates to this case.

Vogel was amazed that Carla approached him at the bar; she was young and attractive and things like that just didn't happen to him. It now seems likely that it was not the result of some instant attraction to him; I think she sought him out specifically and with a purpose.

I'm not yet sure what that purpose was, but it gives me something to check out. "Sam, I want you to look for other times they might have been together."

"I will, but I have something else to tell you that you might be pleased with."

"I already like that sentence. What is it?"

"In the weeks before her death, Carla made three deposits, one a week, into her checking account. They were for nine thousand dollars each, and she made them in cash."

This is clearly beyond suspicious; she had quit her job and then all of a sudden had this influx of cash. Carla's sister, Linda, had mentioned that she seemed to have come into money. Linda also described something else that now seems suspect: Carla's claim that she was moving out of the house she shared with Linda because she wanted to have some space, to be alone.

Carla was rarely alone. It seems more likely that she wanted to do whatever she was doing away from the potentially watchful eye of Linda.

Something else doesn't jibe. "Sam, do you know if Carla was living alone?"

"I can't be sure, but it seems like it. There's nobody else listed at that address, and the place was quickly re-rented once Carla was reported dead."

Vogel had told me that Carla always wanted them to go to his house to spend the night because she said her roommate was annoying. That seems to have been a lie. There certainly could be nonsinister explanations for it, but considering what else we are learning about Carla, I wouldn't bet on it.

Sam goes back to his office to dig a little more, and I try to think through what I've just learned. It's a little tough to concentrate because Edna keeps screaming at Hike in the other room. I'm better off thinking at home, and discussing the developments with Laurie.

Just before I leave, Sam comes back, an obvious look of excitement on his face.

"Andy, the night that Carla D'Antoni died, when she was pushed off that warehouse roof . . ."

"What about it?"

"She didn't have her phone with her."

"So what?"

"That's why I didn't notice the duplication before."

"What are you talking about, Sam?

"Andy, Bledsoe, and Phillips were both there that night. They were at the warehouse where Carla D'Antoni died."

Pharmacon had their IPO today."

The caller reporting this news is Edna's cousin Freddie, who is my stockbroker. I had asked him to let me know when it happened.

"How did it do?"

"Well, it was all presold. They went out at ten dollars a share, which brought them a little over six hundred million. The stock has since gone down a bit, but not much. It's trading now at nine eighty. Surprisingly there's been very little volume."

"What does that mean?"

"That the people who bought it are holding on. Usually when an IPO hits the market, the trading volume on the stock is heavy."

"So would the Pharmacon people be happy today?"

"They're not tossing confetti, but it has to be what they expected. They've brought in money to allow them to go forward, but this is not a ringing endorsement."

"Thanks, Freddie."

As I hang up, I get a text from Robby Divine. It simply says, "I told you so."

He did tell me it would not do well, and Alex Vogel said the same thing. Robby was saying it as an outside potential investor;

Alex was an insider, so he was reluctant to get into specifics as to why he felt that way.

It doesn't matter to me much, unless Vogel was planning to use it as a windfall to pay his legal bills. Either way, I have more important issues to focus on.

I believe that Bledsoe and Phillips murdered Carla D'Antoni. It is beyond any conception of coincidence that they just happened to be in the neighborhood, walking past the warehouse, when Carla fell to her death. One of them pushed her; it doesn't matter which one.

We're not going to get them charged and convicted for doing what they did; their own deaths provided them with an unwanted get-out-of-jail-free card. So we have to focus on why. I don't think that there is any doubt they were hired to do it; the fact that they were murdered proves conclusively that someone was above them, someone who sent them on their missions. One of those missions was to kill Alex Vogel.

Whatever organization it is that is running all this, the job security is not all that great. Phillips and Bledsoe were employees who were terminated in the literal sense. I also think Carla fits that definition.

That she was with Bledsoe in that bar for two hours would seem to show that they had a relationship, probably a working one, that only went sour later.

I also believe that part of her employment was to develop a relationship with Alex Vogel, though I don't yet know why. The list of things that I don't yet know is long.

There is a list of things that are essential. We need to find out who Phillips and Bledsoe were working for, and why they were directed to commit those killings. We also need to rattle someone's cage; we can't sit back and talk theory anymore. The trial is approaching.

Laurie and I discuss this, and I say, "Sam told us that Phillips and Bledsoe hung out most nights at the Masters Bar, so that's where we have to start."

"Who are you referring to when you say 'we'?"

"I am referring to me."

"And me, and Corey, and most definitely Marcus."

"We can't walk in there like the Rose Bowl Parade."

"True. But our float has to be at least somewhat impressive" is her counter.

Laurie and I both know where this is going to end up, so my choice is either to continue to jockey for unnecessary position or go right to the endgame.

I'm not in a jockeying mood, so I simply say, "Marcus."

She nods. "Deal. Now let's talk about what you want to accomplish. Then we can work on the 'how.'"

Laurie calls Marcus and Corey to come over, and I go out to get pizza. Corey brings Simon Garfunkel with him, which is not a news event. He brings Simon pretty much everywhere; Simon is clearly his best friend, as well as a valuable member of the K Team.

We don't invite Hike to the meeting. It has nothing to do with the legal side of things, and none of us would enjoy Hike telling us that our approach is not going to work, and that we're all going to die in a hail of bullets.

I do have Sam Willis join us because I have a specific plan for him.

Simon opts not to sit in on our planning session; he and Tara have become fast friends, and they go off to play with Tara's toys and sniff each other. Sebastian also likes Simon, so much so that he actually wakes up for a few minutes when Simon arrives.

Once we clear away the pizza plates, I set the strategic table. "I'm not going into this bar to learn about these two guys.

People who know them are not going to break into a spontaneous version of 'Bledsoe and Phillips . . . this is your life.' If anyone cares about me, the prevailing attitude will be distrust and dislike."

"You keep saying 'I' and 'me,'" Laurie points out. "You're not going in there alone. We've had this conversation."

"Right. Marcus will be there, but I don't think they should know we're together. Okay, Marcus?"

"Yunnhh." Marcus is a man of few words, and the ones he does say are completely impossible to understand by anybody other than Laurie. But more than possibly anyone else I know, he manages to get his meaning across.

I lay out the plan and we kick it around for a while. Corey has a couple of suggestions, which everyone agrees make it better. The whole discussion takes less than twenty minutes.

We're ready to go.

I'm not sure how I would characterize Masters Bar and Grill. For one thing, it's much more bar than grill. They serve food, though the menu is limited to the basics, but patrons basically go there to drink. Certainly nothing about it is fancy or genteel; definitely not the kind of place you would go in and order a piña colada or a cosmopolitan.

It's not a welcoming place for nonregulars, although there is no overt intimidation. Newcomers can come in and have a quiet drink without being bothered, and no brawl or gunfight is likely to break out.

There's a pool table near the back and an old-fashioned jukebox. I wouldn't describe it as a particularly tough place, although it is not in what would be considered a safe neighborhood. Most of the patrons are men, and most look like they can handle themselves if they needed to.

The bartender is maybe fifty years old and seems like he is coming up on his fiftieth anniversary of working here. It has probably been years since he smiled, and one does not seem imminent.

I time my arrival at Masters for nine fifteen. No particular reason; it just doesn't feel too early or too late. As always, I would describe myself as more than nervous but less than petrified. I would much rather describe myself as retired.

Nobody turns to look at me as I walk in. Two of the patrons who don't look are Sam Willis and Marcus Clark. They are not sitting together; Sam is at a table not far from the bar, and Marcus is across the room, near the window.

Sam has his elbows resting on the table, a signal that he has accomplished what I sent him in there to do. He's not smiling, but I'll bet he's having a tough time avoiding it. Sam has long wanted to be in on the action, and this must be scratching that itch.

I walk up to the bar and say to the bartender, "Hey, how ya doin'?" That is my version of Andy Carpenter street talk.

The bartender is apparently disinclined to tell me how he's doing, so all he says is "You drinking?"

"My name is Andy Carpenter. I'm a lawyer."

"You drinking or not?"

"What do you have on tap?"

"Beer."

"That'll work. I'm looking for information about Orlando Bledsoe and Charlie Phillips."

He reacts slightly, but then masks it. "Try Google."

"I don't think so. I'm trying you."

"Never heard of them."

"Really? Because they came in here all the time. And one of the times they were joined by Carla D'Antoni. That wasn't too long before they killed her."

"Get lost."

"If I get lost, within an hour you'll be hosting a cop convention in here. So you may just be an asshole who doesn't know anything, but I'll bet you know people who do know something." I'm trying to sound tough, but it's a stretch for me. I'm considered closer to Mr. Rogers than Mr. T.

He walks over to a landline phone behind the bar and picks it up. He dials a number, then has a conversation that I can't hear that lasts about a minute.

He hangs up and comes back to me. "Tomorrow night . . . ten o'clock. Come here and go around the back. There's a door that leads to an office; go in there."

"Who am I meeting?"

"Tomorrow night . . . ten o'clock. Come here and go around the back. There's a door that leads to an office; go in there."

"You're quite a conversationalist, you know?"

"Now get lost."

That sounds like a reasonably good idea, so that's what I do.

Technically, we have probably already gotten what we are after.

Sam had gotten to the bar well before I did and performed his task brilliantly.

We expected that the bartender would make a phone call to get instructions on how he should handle the pain-in-the-ass lawyer. We thought the call would probably be made after I left, but it took place while I was there.

When Sam sat down, he called the listed number for the place, to confirm that the phone behind the bar was the one with that number. He watched as the bartender answered the ringing phone. That identified the phone number that the bartender would, we hoped, later use to make the call.

Sam also struck up a conversation with the bartender and got his name. That way, Sam could also get his cell number, if that was the phone he used to make the call. It turned out not to be necessary.

Now Sam can access the bar phone records and know who received the call. That will bring us at least one step further up the ladder to the people behind Phillips and Bledsoe. We should get a report from Sam with the name later today or tomorrow morning.

Mission accomplished.

And yet . . .

The offer of a meeting tonight is a potential opportunity to learn more and to possibly get a firsthand look at one or more people in the conspiracy. It's entirely possible, maybe even probable, that nothing positive would come out of it, but there's always that chance.

Laurie, Marcus, Corey, Sam, and I meet to discuss the pros and cons. We sit in the kitchen eating blueberry muffins and drinking coffee. "What do you think they have in mind?" I ask of no one in particular.

Corey provides the answer. "It depends what they are going to do. If they're planning to kill you, then you might meet someone significant. They're meeting because they want information, and that would require someone smart enough and high up enough to ask the right questions. But if you are going to get a look at someone like that, then the plan would be to kill you before you could reveal it.

"If they're just going to smack you around and intimidate you, then you won't meet anyone important."

I nod. "Then I hope they kill me. This might be a meeting I shouldn't attend."

"Or you could meet and we could prevent them from killing you," Laurie says. "Or even smacking you around. Hopefully."

"We go in, in force. They won't know what hit them," Sam says. No one responds or even looks at him. It's as if he didn't say it. If an accountant says words in a kitchen and no one listens, did he make a sound?

Instead, everyone turns to Marcus. "Marcus, can we do this?" Laurie asks. "Keeping Andy alive is sort of important to me."

"And me," I say. "Are we confident about this?"

Marcus gives a slight nod. "Ynnhh."

"Okay. Good," Laurie says, which must mean that Marcus said he was on board. Then she turns to me. "But it's ultimately your call, Andy. You're the only one that can do this."

I have been through this kind of thing a number of times before. Lawyers shouldn't be in physical danger, which is one of the reasons I became a lawyer. But I am frequently in a hell of a lot of danger, which is one of the reasons I want to become an ex-lawyer.

In these situations, I think of Marcus as an airplane. When I fly, I don't stop to worry that I am sitting in a chair thirty-five thousand feet in the air with nothing under me. I don't know how it stays up there, but I don't ask questions. I trust the airplane to prevent me from plummeting to my death.

It's the same with Marcus. I don't fully know how he does what he does, but I completely trust him to do it. I put myself in his hands, and even though I usually approach piss-in-my-pants terror, I never question that decision.

And he always comes through.

So far.

"Let's do it," I say. "But, Marcus, if I get killed, I'm going to be really pissed off. And you don't want to have to deal with a pissed-off Andy Carpenter."

So once again we plan an operation that I wish I was not a part of. I would much rather not be indispensable.

One of my long-term, retirement goals is dispensability.

The calendar being what it is, I can't afford to waste a day. So while my preference would be to spend today curled in the fetal position dreading the meeting at the bar tonight, I need to get some things done.

Sam and Marcus are off checking to make sure our plan has a chance of working, while I am about to set a record for the most consecutive unproductive meetings in one building. I'm back at Pharmacon to interview Jordan Tucker.

Tucker was Robert Giarrusso's boss at Pharmacon. By all accounts Giarrusso was a biochemistry genius, so his boss must be on another mental planet.

Not so much.

"I'm more of an executive running the department," Tucker tells me early on in our conversation. "My background is in biochemistry, sure, but I am not in Giarrusso's class. That is a very small class."

"There seems to be a general feeling here that he was going to leave." I don't mention that I know that to be the case, since Vogel confirmed it.

"Doesn't surprise me. On the one hand, I'm surprised he stayed as long as he did. He wanted the autonomy of running his own show. And the truth is, he deserved it."

"What's the other hand?"

"We were able to provide him with state-of-the-art facilities, the capital to do his work, and enough capable people around to assist him."

"And you aren't surprised he would walk away from that?"

Tucker shakes his head. "My guess is that Robert was onto something that he wasn't anxious to share."

"What kind of something?"

"Robert had a lab in his home; he referred to himself as the mad doctor with the laboratory in the basement. We helped him set it up. Business hours weren't terribly important to him; he worked whenever he had the inspiration, which was often. I wouldn't be shocked if he came up with some promising idea for a drug that he didn't want to become a product of this company."

"But you don't know the details?"

Another shake of the head. "I don't even know that I'm right. It's just my best guess. If I am right, it makes his death that much more of a tragedy, because if Robert thought that highly of the drug, then it's a shame it died with him."

"Nobody knows what it was or had his notes?"

Tucker shrugs. "I don't."

"You know of any enemies he had?"

Tucker shakes his head. "Hard to imagine he had any. He really didn't hang around with people much at all. So I don't know what anyone could have had against him."

"Have you replaced him?"

"We're in the process of hiring two people. They're good, but combined they won't be able to replace him."

Fresh off that unenlightening interview, I head down to the jail. I think Vogel could clear up a couple of things I'm curious about.

When he's brought in, he seems even more stressed than the previous times I've seen him. "Are you okay?"

"I guess so. I'm just real tired of being here. And they're treating me like I'm in danger; I'm not allowed to interact with the other prisoners very much, and when I do, they watch me like a hawk."

"You should be flattered."

"I'm not. Although I have a feeling I wouldn't have that much in common with my colleagues here."

"I have a couple of questions for you. Did Carla know you were going out on the boat that day?"

He has to think about this for a while. Then, "Definitely, yes. I remember she wanted to come along, but I said that it was business."

"How far in advance would that conversation have been?"

He shrugs. "Hard to say, but probably at least a few days. It wasn't a spur-of-the-moment trip, and it was a Saturday, so I would have been letting her know we weren't going to be together that day."

"You told me that Carla wanted to spend nights at your house rather than hers because her roommate was annoying."

"Right."

"She didn't have a roommate."

His surprise is evident on his face. "I don't understand."

I'm going to be upfront with him about this. It's not necessary for his defense, but he should know the truth. "Alex, your relationship with her appears to be very different than you believed it was. She was using you; she was employed by the people who tried to kill you, and who wound up killing her."

"Are you sure?" He seems stunned by the news.

"I'm sure."

He doesn't say anything for a full twenty seconds, then grins a small, embarrassed grin. "Well, I guess that explains my sudden appeal to women. But why would she make that up about a roommate?"

"Maybe she had a reason for wanting to be in your house. Maybe she was trying to figure out the lay of the land. We need to find out what was taken in that theft."

"I never went back there during the three weeks I was in hiding; I was afraid Russo's people might be watching it. I hadn't even known about the break-in."

"The police executed a search warrant on it; that's how they found the explosive traces. Based on the discovery, the police didn't take much of consequence. The more important question is what did the thieves take."

"I didn't have anything of real value. I didn't keep cash in the house, no jewelry or expensive artwork." He pauses. "Damn, have someone check the filing cabinet in the closet in my upstairs office. It was always locked."

"What was in there?"

"Work papers. They could be valuable, depending on who got hold of them."

"Why would they be valuable? What kind of papers?" When it comes to information about his work, Vogel can be reluctant to share.

"Well, there was a lot of my own work . . . research results, progress in dealing with the FDA . . . that wouldn't mean much to anyone and there are duplicates at Pharmacon. But there was also . . . there was a great deal of information about the new drug Robert Giarrusso was developing. It was very promising, though you can never be sure until you get into the testing protocols. But it was the reason we were starting our company."

I had a feeling that was what he was going to say. "I'll get on it right away. I'll stop at your house on the way home."

"There's a key in the garage; it's taped under the circuit-breaker box."

I leave and go straight for Vogel's house. From outside it looks normal except that the grass is in serious need of a trimming. I imagine the neighbors are starting to get annoyed.

The key is where Vogel said it was, and I use it to open the front door. The house is a mess; either the thieves were ransacking the place or wanted it to look like they were.

I walk around the downstairs but don't know what I'm looking for. The thieves tore up the place pretty well, but I can't say what if anything was taken because I have no idea what was there in the first place.

In the mess I see a bunch of dog toys; when I leave, I'll take them with me and bring them to Aggie. She might be attached to them and they might remind her of Vogel.

A downstairs room seems like a workroom, with tools and pieces of wood and metal. It's the kind of room a real man who can build things might have, the kind of room that I will never have any use for. This must be where they found the traces of explosives.

I go upstairs and the first room I see is the bedroom, which is in the same disarray as the downstairs. Nothing to be learned in here.

Next I reach the office and walk past the mess on the floor to get to the closet. The door to it is closed, which seems unusual in this environment. Based on the look of the rest of the house, the thieves would certainly have opened it and looked inside, and they wouldn't likely have closed it. They were unconcerned with appearances and made no effort to leave the place presentable.

I open the door and look inside. I have no idea if the filing cabinet is still locked or not because there is no filing cabinet.

Everything seems to be in place.

Sam has rented an office in the building across the alley from the back of the bar. From the window he can observe all the comings and goings and even has a sight line into the office where I assume the meeting will take place.

He had to rent it for three months; that was the minimum. It was two thousand a month, so it cost us six grand for a place we are going to use for six hours. Ritz-Carltons come a hell of a lot cheaper, and they leave chocolates on the pillow at night.

Sam has been there most of the day, but has not reported much activity. A couple of people have come into the office briefly and then left. One of them is the bartender, which I take as significant. If there is an indoor way to move from the bar to the office, then their wanting me to enter through the back alley feels ominous.

About a half hour before the meeting time, Sam texts the rest of the team members that three guys have set up shop outside the entrance in the alley. It's another significant development and reassures me that we are not overpreparing for what might be a nonevent. Of course, I am definitely still rooting for a non-event.

Sam types, probably in an understatement, that the three

guys "look like they can handle themselves." Then he adds, "If need be, I can definitely pick them off from here."

Before I can respond, Laurie beats me to it, typing, "Sam, you brought your gun?" If there was an emoji face that conveyed total horror, I am sure Laurie would have added it.

His response is "Just in case," and she comes back with "Sam, take the bullets out of the gun, just in case."

With the knowledge that I will be met at the door, we make our final decisions. Marcus will be with me. If they just let us in, fine. If they attempt to do anything violent, or if they insist that I go in alone, then Marcus will deal with them. My role will be to stand aside and attempt to preserve my manly dignity.

Corey Douglas will also be in the alley, about fifty yards away, pretending to be casually walking Simon. They will move in if necessary, as will Laurie, who will be in a parked car around the corner and out of sight.

Sam set up my phone so that one press of a button will send an emergency text to everyone, should that be necessary.

We have the option of driving into the alley or parking on the street and walking there. Marcus opts for walking; I have no idea why and I don't care. Marcus calls the shots.

So we park a block and a half away, passing Laurie in the car as we walk toward the alley. As we reach it, we see the three men standing casually in the doorway. They don't look worried, nor does Marcus. I'm worried enough for all of us.

When we're about fifty yards away, I see Corey at the other end of the alley, walking Simon. They will gradually move closer as we make contact with the three goons waiting for us.

As we reach them, I smile and say, "Top of the evening to you, lads."

It seems like in every "gathering of goons" one of them is

the designated talker, and it's always the guy in the middle. I don't think it's necessarily a sign of some kind of hierarchy; my guess is they are all equal in rank. Maybe they have a meeting beforehand and draw straws. But one talks and the other guys' role in communications is to nod their support for whatever Middle Goon is saying.

In this case, Middle Goon says, "Where are you going?"

I think it's obvious to everyone where we're going, but I say, "Into the office to talk to your boss."

"You," Middle Goon says, then points to Marcus. "Not him."

"He's my stenographer; I want to have a transcript of our meeting."

"What the hell are you talking about?"

"Which part didn't you understand?"

"You go inside. You"—Middle Goon points to Marcus—"beat it."

I have been in these situations with Marcus before. Usually he waits for the adversary to make the first move, but on rare occasions he moves first. I think he makes the decision based on whether he believes violence is inevitable, as well as an instinctive assessment of how much danger we're facing.

I'm not sure what happens in this case. I think I see Left Goon and Right Goon make almost imperceptible moves toward us. Maybe Marcus sees it as well. Or maybe he just wants to get an advantage. Or maybe he wants us to quickly clear the area before Sam accidentally shoots one of us.

But Marcus doesn't hesitate. He takes advantage of the leaning side goons first. He throws a left into the side of Right Goon's head, turning him in the other direction, then throws an equally devastating right to Left Goon's temple, reversing his trajectory as well. The crunching sounds are awful or wonderful, depending on one's perspective.

Gravity takes over in both cases, and their unconscious heads hit the cement along with the rest of their bodies. Middle Goon looks surprised; this was the last thing he expected.

It is also the last thing he sees, at least for the rest of the evening. Marcus kicks him in the groin, then generously spares him the pain of it by knocking him unconscious with an upper-cut as he bends forward. He lands on top of Left Goon, though I am positive that neither is aware of it.

Marcus motions to me, and I follow him into the building. Before I do, I see that Corey and Simon have almost reached us. They will stand guard over the three goons and keep them from reentering the fray, in the unlikely event that any of them gain consciousness anytime soon.

I'm sure Laurie will join them as well. I hope Sam doesn't.

Round one to the good guys.

recognize the guy sitting behind the desk: Tony Lynch.

He's called Big Tony because he's big and because the Joseph Russo crime family puts pathetically little effort into coming up with creative nicknames.

I met Big Tony because he was in the room when I went to see Joseph Russo, Sr., on another case. I remember him because when I was leaving, he told me that if I caused any more trouble, he would put a bullet in my head and dump me in the Passaic River. Certain conversations just stick in your mind.

Big Tony doesn't greet us with a welcoming smile, but rather a look of surprise. "How did you get in here?"

"Down the alley, through the door, and into this office. It's not brain surgery, Tony."

"My guys out there?"

"Three big dumb-looking guys? Yeah, we passed them on the way in. I invited them to the meeting, but they preferred to stay unconscious on the cement. By the way, have you met Marcus Clark?"

Big Tony's look of surprise has been replaced by one of, if not fear, then concern. I don't know if he's heard of Marcus, or if, more likely, he realizes that anyone who put down three of his guys is a force that he will be unable to reckon with. "Get out of here."

"Tony, I've got a feeling that you may not spend much time at Mensa meetings. We are in charge here, not you."

"I've got nothing to say to you. So you might as well get out now. I've got more people on the way."

"Are they as tough as the three clowns sleeping outside? Tony, you don't want us to leave, because if we do, you're coming with us. And you will never be heard from again. You killed people, Tony, defenseless people. So whatever happens to you, you deserve it."

"I didn't kill anybody."

"Phillips and Bledsoe did. And you gave the order."

"No."

"Then who did? Russo?"

"I've got nothing to say."

"Your decision. Let's go."

Marcus walks toward him, and Big Tony, whose new nickname should be Little Brain, winds up to take a punch at him. Marcus intercepts and grabs hold of Tony's arm and uses it to toss Tony at least seven feet, into a wall. It's as if he turned Tony into a discus, the only difference being that a discus doesn't scream in pain.

"Your intelligence level continues to unimpress," I say. "Okay, we ready now? Time to go."

Marcus walks over to Tony to coax him, but Tony wants no part of him. "Russo is not giving the orders."

"Who is?"

"If he finds out I gave him up, I'm a dead man walking."

"Then he won't."

"Victor," Tony says with obvious reluctance.

"And who might he be?"

"He's some foreign guy. Russian or one of those European shitholes. Thick accent. Russo told me to do whatever he says."

"What's his last name?"

"I don't know. I've never seen him; he calls me and tells me what to do."

"So on his orders you sent Phillips and Bledsoe out to kill Carla D'Antoni and blow up that boat."

"No, not me. That must have been someone else."

"Yeah, it was the murder fairy. Why were Phillips and Bledsoe killed?"

"I wasn't involved in that, but I would assume it was because they screwed up. The hit was supposed to be on that Vogel guy."

I'm sure Tony's lying about not giving the order for the murders, but it doesn't matter right now. I'm not going to try to convict him here; my goal is to learn. I do believe he is taking his orders and sending them down the line. "Why is all this being done?"

"I don't know; I swear. I just know there's big money in it, enough to go around for everybody. I heard Russo say he's going to make a fortune."

I press Tony for more information; but if he's got any, he's not giving it up. I wrap it up with "Last night, when the bartender called you, what did he say?"

"That you were asking questions and I'd want to know about it."

I asked the question that way because I wanted Tony's phone number. If I asked for it, he'd be on the alert. So my confirming that the bartender called him was good enough because Sam is going to get the number. Hopefully that will lead us to Victor.

We leave and find Corey, Laurie, and Simon Garfunkel keeping an eye on the three fallen warriors. "Let's go," I say. "Fun time is over."

"Now?" Corey asks. "We have a bet on which guy will wake up first."

As if on cue, the guy lying on the left moans and moves a couple of inches. "Damn," Laurie says. "Simon, you win again."

We now know a number of important things.

We know that Alex Vogel did not kill Mellman and Giarrusso because we know who did. It was Bledsoe and Phillips. We also know that they killed Carla D'Antoni.

We know that they were directed to do so by Big Tony, who was given the initial order by someone else. We also know that Joseph Russo, Jr., is involved; his fingerprints are all over everything.

We also believe other things but aren't certain about them. One of those is that Robert Giarrusso's new drug idea is considered so valuable that all these killings have been done in pursuit of it.

We believe that Russo will profit from all of this, since he has essentially been loaning out his people in support of it. We also believe that Tony was telling the truth about taking his orders from a man named Victor; it seems unlikely that Tony would have had the smarts to make up that story in the moment.

We believe that Carla D'Antoni was part of the conspiracy, possibly on loan from Russo like the others. She probably died because she learned too much, so once she accomplished her mission, she was deemed too risky to keep around.

Unfortunately, what we know and believe has no value in the

legal world we are operating in. We not only can't prove any of it, we probably can't even demonstrate to the judge that it is worthwhile for the jury to hear and consider.

But it does have value in the investigative world. It gives us insights, which in turn provides more to go on as we dig to find evidence that we can use in court.

So it's back to the jail for me to talk with my client. He's got some information he has not yet fully shared with me. He's going to now. "Tell me about Giarrusso's new drug," I say as soon as we sit down.

"Why is that important?"

"Because I say it is, and I'm your lawyer." He's pissing me off. "This trial is about to start, and if I tell you I need something, then your job is to do whatever you can to get it for me. Otherwise you're going to spend a lot of years in a small cell regretting that you didn't."

"Okay." I think he's getting the message, but I'm about to find out for sure. "I was just being protective of it. Our business depends on secrecy. If this gets out, then someone else can steal it, and Robert's family should be the ones to profit from it. And since it wasn't patented, it could easily be stolen. But I'll tell you whatever I can."

"What's it for?"

"Alzheimer's. Robert believed it could add five or ten years of productive life when the disease was diagnosed early enough."

"How does it work?"

"I don't know; that's not my area. But in general terms, I think it somehow helps the body's natural defenses against it. I really can't be specific; I'm not a scientist. But Robert was incredibly excited about it; it was why we were enthusiastic about starting our own company. He was overly enthusiastic, though, and I tried to calm him down."

"Is that what you argued about that day, getting onto the boat?"

"Like I said, I really don't remember. It could have been, but if it was, that wouldn't have been anywhere near the first time. He didn't have a full understanding of what was necessary to bring a drug to market, financially and research-wise."

"But you do?"

"Not completely. I only know my own area. Stephen Mellman understood the financial end, and he and I tried to get Robert to be patient. It wasn't easy for him; he had an idea that he thought could help millions of suffering people, and we were telling him how much time it was going to take. I understood his frustration, but I deal in the reality."

"Join the club."

"Why are you so interested in Robert's drug idea?"

"Because there was no filing cabinet in your closet."

"Are you sure?"

I nod. "I can spot a filing cabinet at fifty feet. Was there anything else in there that could have had this kind of value?"

"No, just work papers, and copies at that. It had to be Robert's work that they wanted."

As I leave, I take a wild shot in the dark. "Does the name Victor mean anything to you?"

"No. Who is he?"

"Just another question to be answered."

Sam gets basically nowhere with Big Tony's phone.

A number of calls were made to a burner phone that we assume to be Victor's, and they line up pretty well with the dates of the boat explosion and the murder of Carla D'Antoni.

Unfortunately, that burner phone has been either discarded or destroyed, and the only calls it had ever received were from Big Tony. It had never made any outgoing calls and did not have a GPS in it.

Victor, assuming he exists and that is his name, appears to walk on the smart side of the street. I doubt that's where he ran into Big Tony.

I need to learn more about him, or at least about the possibility of him. Corey Douglas is good friends with Lieutenant Romeo Guttierez of the New Jersey State Police, and Corey has set up this meeting for me. Lieutenant Guttierez's area of expertise is organized crime in northern New Jersey, and he has proven fairly effective in attacking it.

"Corey says you're a pain in the ass." As icebreakers go, Guttierez's could use some work.

"Yet he worships the ground I walk on."

"That's not how he describes it. But he asked me to talk to you, so talk."

"I have reason to believe that someone who talks with an accent, maybe Russian, maybe Ukrainian, maybe whatever, is using Joseph Russo, Jr.'s men with the full cooperation of Joseph Russo, Jr."

"Do you know the someone's name?"

"Victor. Hopefully you know him? Maybe double-dated with him in high school?"

Guttierez shakes his head. "Never heard of him. What is he using Russo's men for?"

"Murders. At least three and counting."

That gets his attention. "Okay, what do you want to know?"

"Let's start with whether it makes sense that Russo would hand over his people to anyone."

"Depends on the money involved. It would take a lot."

"It feels like there's money all over this thing."

"My bet is on Victor being Russian."

"Why?"

"Because we're being invaded. The Russian Mafia decided a few years ago that there were a limited number of rubles to steal over there, plus they had to share it with members of the government. So they decided this was the promised land.

"They brought seed money with them, and that was perfect timing. Because organized crime here hit a money crunch, and Russo's family happens to be the crunchiest. So it wouldn't surprise me if they sought outside funding, and the Russians have it big-time."

"So how does this work?"

"Think of it as a big business. . . . They want to expand into new markets, so they buy their way in. Take Amazon as an example. They wanted to become a grocery chain, but they didn't start a business and build stores. They bought Whole Foods, and, presto, they're in. Then they start giving out discounts, and pretty soon my wife is feeding me kale. But that's another story."

"So the Russians are buying Russo's business?"

Guttierez shakes his head. "Not yet. First they link up with him; they pay him for his people. Then when they're entrenched, with all their money Russo's people become theirs, and Russo either goes along or follows his father to the promised land."

I describe in the barest terms the situation with Robert Giarrusso's drug and ask if that is the kind of business the Russians might be interested in getting into.

"Doesn't sound like it. But if the money is big enough, you never know."

I thank Guttierez and ask him if I can come back with more questions, should they come up.

"Sure. And if you find out more about this Victor, definitely come back. If he is actually Russian Mafia, you do not want to deal with him."

"He's dangerous; I hear you."

"Dangerous doesn't go near it. These people make Russo and his guys look like a charm-school class."

'm spending so much time at Pharmacon, they're going to give me a gold watch.

I need to know more about drugs, and except for Pharmacon, my only connection to the industry is buying Aleve at Walgreens. But I buy a lot of it; lawyering gives me a headache.

My first stop is Eric Buckner, the CEO. I don't have anything to talk to him about, but he's the head guy, so I think it's right to tell him I'm still hanging around.

"If it'll help Alex Vogel, go for it," he says.

Going for it means talking to two executives that I've already met with. The first is Gerald Bennings, the CFO and former boss of one of the murder victims, Stephen Mellman.

"You're back," he says, when I barge in on him.

"That would be tough to deny."

"I'm pretty busy. Can we do this quickly?"

I nod. "We can. Here's a hypothetical. There's an idea for a new drug, potentially revolutionary. Someone steals it, and—"

"In this hypothetical, was it patented?"

"No."

He frowns. "Stupid." Then, "Go on."

"Once it was stolen, for it to realize its value, it would have to come to market in a normal manner, wouldn't it?"

"What do you mean?"

"I mean testing, FDA approval, that process. It could never be mass marketed any other way, could it?"

"No, that's the only way I know of, if they want to make real money. Some black-market presence wouldn't do it."

"So they would have to raise money?"

He shrugs. "They'd have to spend money. I don't know about raising it; they might already have it. Depends on the company."

"So it could go through an existing company or start-up?"

He nods. "Right."

"Can that be done in any kind of secrecy?"

"Only up to a point. Once they started their testing protocol, it would involve doctors, hospitals, labs . . . pretty hard to keep that a secret."

"Would it come up on your radar?"

"Me personally? Only if they were out there raising money. Then I would definitely hear about it, or I wasn't doing my job. If they didn't raise money, then I imagine Jordan Tucker would be the one to talk to."

I nod. "I'm bothering him next." I met with Tucker previously as well; he's the scientist who was Robert Giarrusso's boss. Before I go, I ask the question I ask everybody: "Have you heard the name Victor? Maybe someone you know through business?"

He thinks for a moment. "No."

Victor obviously does not get around much.

I stop in next at Jordan Tucker's office. He looks at his watch and tells me he's busy and could I hurry it up.

With cell phones proliferating and telling time, I think the main reason to own a watch these days is as a way to show someone that you have little time for them. Looking at a cell phone doesn't convey the same message; the person you're trying to get rid of might think you're just reading a text or an email.

Jordan agrees that he'd be the one most likely to know about a revolutionary new drug, but that nothing in recent weeks seems to fit that bill. I ask him to keep his eyes out for one, specifically an Alzheimer's drug, and he looks at me like I'm an idiot, but agrees as a way to get me out of his office.

Then he checks his watch again, just in case he forgot what it said a minute ago.

I'm out of here.

t was a beautiful spring day. Very little wind, no chance of rain.

A perfect day to be out on a boat, in the ocean.

Norman Trell begins his opening statement to the jury this way. He's setting the idyllic scene before transitioning to what everyone in the courtroom knows is the horror to come.

"The defendant, Alex Vogel, owned a boat that he kept on Long Beach Island, New Jersey. There will be testimony that he used it fairly often, basically every weekend that the weather permitted. So it was no surprise to anyone that he was going out on the water that day.

"There will also be testimony that he was accompanied by two other people, business colleagues of his. Their names were Stephen Mellman and Robert Giarrusso. There is no evidence that they had been on the defendant's boat before; they may have been, but we just don't know.

"Yes, I will be the first to admit that there are things we don't know. For another example, we know that they were arguing about something as they boarded the boat, but we don't know what the argument was about.

"That's what happens in situations like this. Three people were there; now two are dead and the person who killed them is the only one who knows all the details. But that's all they are . . . details. We know more than enough to see the big picture.

"One thing we do know for sure is that it was the last time Stephen Mellman and Robert Giarrusso were on Alex Vogel's boat. That is because an explosion completely destroyed it. They were no doubt killed instantly, and their bodies were never found. They were lost at sea.

"But Alex Vogel did not die that day; he is sitting right here. Alex Vogel left that boat before the explosion; testimony will explain how he did that. But did he come forward after his apparent brush with death and tell what happened? Did he report that his friends had died on his boat? No, he stayed hidden, and to this day has not spoken to the police.

"There is something called consciousness of guilt. That is a legal term, and it will be explained to you. But basically it means that someone acted as if guilty, and the judge will tell you that you consider it as you would circumstantial evidence. Alex Vogel did that in spades.

"There is also additional forensic evidence which will contribute to what is proof beyond a reasonable doubt that Alex Vogel deliberately and with premeditation turned that beautiful day on the ocean into a nightmare of death.

"You don't have to take my word for it, nor should you. Mr. Carpenter and I are advocates; nothing we say is actual evidence. But you will get to hear and see the actual evidence, and I have no doubt you will come to the conclusion that Alex Vogel is guilty as charged.

"Thank you."

Judge Mahomes asks me if I want to give my statement now or hold it until the start of the defense case. I never defer; this is not like winning the toss at the beginning of a football game. I want to get on the record now that we have a case, and that we will be a force to be reckoned with.

Trell's style is to stand behind a podium and speak from there; mine is to walk around. I feel like I make a connection with the jury that way, and it also gives me my only chance to exercise.

We spent a day and a half picking the jury, and I have no idea how well we did. I won't know for sure until they deliver their verdict, but either way it's too late to do anything about it now.

This jury consists of seven women and five men. There are five Caucasians, five Hispanics, and two African Americans. The one thing that they all have in common is that they couldn't figure out a way to get out of jury duty.

"Ladies and gentlemen, I would like you to imagine a situation I sincerely hope you will never be in. Someone has just tried to kill you, and in the process killed two of your friends. You escaped because you were lucky, and you were smart.

"But you saw the brutality, and you know that it is you that they were really after. What do you do?

"Well, the smart thing is to go to the police. But what if you think they can't protect you? What if you know who is after you, and know that they have the resources and the ruthlessness to come after you again and again until they succeed in killing you?

"Is it so crazy to think that in a situation like that you might hide? And if the world thinks you had died, and more importantly if the killers think you had died, wouldn't you want to keep them thinking that until you could figure out what to do?

"If you were panicked and afraid, isn't it possible you might make a bad decision? Or maybe try and buy time until you could make a good one?

"Alex Vogel is a successful businessman. Mr. Trell will not

point to any previous violence in his life because there hasn't been any. He has always been a respected member of society.

"He's given his time and money to countless charitable causes to make our city and our country a better place. He is a veteran who saw combat and was honored for his efforts. None of us have led perfect lives, but Alex Vogel has come closer than most.

"Does it make sense that he would suddenly commit two violent murders and then try and disappear, thereby throwing away everything he had worked so hard for?

"Why? Why would he do that? Maybe Mr. Trell will give us that answer, and we can all wait for him to do that. But I'm betting he doesn't.

"The reason he won't is because no such answer exists. Mr. Vogel is a victim here, first of an attempted murder, and then of a justice system that took the easy route rather than seeking true justice.

"I asked you to imagine yourself in the situation I described. You might have come to a different decision than Mr. Vogel, but your job is not to judge whether he made the correct one. It is to decide if he took the life of his two friends and then effectively ended the life he took so long to build . . . his own life.

"When you came into this courtroom you brought your common sense with you. I simply ask that you use it. Thank you."

Ruth Radford started feeling ill around 6:00 P.M.

It began as a slight headache and a low-grade fever; chills and vomiting began about an hour later. Her husband, Glenn, offered to take her to the emergency room, but she declined. She figured it was just the flu, even though she had gotten her flu shot as the doctor recommended.

By 11:00 P.M. she had gotten much worse, and in the intervening hours, in another upsetting development, Glenn started to experience similar symptoms.

At 3:30 A.M., Glenn decided they needed to get to a hospital. He still felt capable of driving, but he did not know how long that would last. An ambulance was obviously a possibility, but Glenn wanted to get them there himself.

They made it to the small, local hospital, and the emergency-room physician, Dr. Roland Meekins, saw immediately that the situation was urgent. Both of the Radfords had fevers in excess of 103, and Ruth Radford was becoming delirious.

Dr. Meekins began administering antibiotics to the Radfords, then drew blood and called Strickland Labs in Monticello, just eight miles away. He reached the lab director, Allen Julian, at home. He had met Julian on a number of occasions, including once since Julian had taken over the top position after the untimely death of his boss, Jeremy Bowers.

Julian agreed to rush into the lab and do an immediate culture on the blood sample that Meekins was having messengered over. Julian did so, and he delivered shocking news. The Radfords had contracted *Diveria aureus.*

Diveria aureus, Julian knew, was one of the new breed of antibiotic-resistant superbugs that was striking fear into medical scientists all over the world. He knew of only a few cases in the United States, but was aware that a drug was currently being tested to deal with it.

That drug was in advanced testing, and the protocol allowed Julian and the attending physicians to acquire it and administer it. So Julian called the company, Pharmacon, and apprised them of the emergency. Per the protocol, the company agreed to get the drug, Loraxil, there as fast as humanly possible.

Loraxil had been in Phase 3 testing for six months, and Pharmacon had presented impressive test results to the FDA, but more work and testing was still to be done. The company was hopeful, but the FDA was not yet granting permission to go forward. The FDA was being careful and could take time since no pressing medical need had to be met.

Both Julian and Pharmacon, having put this in motion, then called the CDC, which sprang into action and sent one of its scientists to examine the Strickland Labs sample and culture, to make sure that proper procedures were being followed. The FDA also sent its people to the lab and hospital to deal with what was obviously an urgent matter.

Within six hours the experimental Pharmacon drug, Loraxil, was in the hands of Meekins and his colleagues. Four hours after that, it became clear that the drug was working, the Radfords were showing some improvement.

The government scientists arriving at Strickland Labs confirmed that Julian had correctly conducted the cultures and that the Radfords' blood samples were positive for *Diveria aureus*.

By the next morning the Radfords had made a dramatic recovery and were deemed out of danger.

The Pharmacon drug, Loraxil, had done its magic.

Trell's first witness is Detective Sergeant Mike Gerdes, a New Jersey State Police homicide detective.

Trell quickly establishes date and time, then asks Gerdes how he first learned about the boat explosion.

"I was in my office and we received a call from the Coast Guard about the reported incident."

"Who reported it to them?"

"There was a boat nearby when it exploded. They notified the Coast Guard, who immediately sent a boat out to investigate. Once they had reason to believe it was a homicide, they called us in."

"And you went out to the scene?"

"I did; I was on call that day. We have our own craft, so I commissioned one and went out there with other members of my team, and a forensics team as well."

"What did you find there?" Trell asks.

"Not much. Some floating wreckage, which the forensics people captured and brought back to shore. No traces of any survivors; nor were there any bodies."

"Did you send any divers down there?"

Gerdes nods. "They followed a short time afterwards, but

as I understand it, the water was too deep and the current too strong for any reasonable chance of finding human remains, and they did not."

"Were you able to interview any witnesses?"

"Yes, the people on the boat that reported the explosion."

"What did you do next?"

"Came back and reported to Captain Shenton, William Shenton. He's in charge of the Homicide Division."

"Thank you. No further questions."

I have little to get from Sergeant Gerdes on cross-examination. He's not an important witness; nothing he said incriminated Alex Vogel, and there is no question that he is telling the truth.

His testimony just starts to set the stage for the key witnesses to follow. But even though the jury will probably not remember or consider anything about his testimony when they deliberate, I need to be careful how I handle him.

I want to make some points, simply to show that we are not rolling over and that we have a case to make. But I don't want to come down hard on him since that will make me look argumentative and badgering. There will be time for that later; doing it now would just irritate the jury and create sympathy for Gerdes.

"Sergeant Gerdes, at the time you were out there on the water, did you have any personal knowledge of what caused the explosion?"

"No."

"But subsequently you came to believe it was an explosive device."

"Yes."

"If there was such a device, do you know who brought it onto the boat?"

"I do not."

"Do you know when it was put on the boat?"

"I don't."

He's a man of few words; when it comes to cross-examinations, I prefer free talkers. "Do you know if it was set off accidentally or intentionally?"

"I couldn't say."

"You couldn't say because you don't know?"

"That's correct."

"If you know, when the boat was docked at the pier on a regular basis, was it somehow locked away? Or could anyone have approached it and even boarded it?"

"It wasn't inaccessible," he says somewhat grudgingly.

"Just to clear up the double negative, are you saying it was accessible?"

"Yes."

"I was there as part of my investigation, and I was able to walk right up to all of the boats, without any guards or anyone there to stop me. Based on your understanding, my experience was not unusual, was it?"

"No."

"Thank you, no further questions."

Next up is Coast Guard captain Peter Lockman, who commanded the ship that was first on the scene after receiving the report from the people on the boat near the explosion.

Captain Lockman has even less to say than Gerdes did, and what little he does say simply repeats Gerdes's testimony. Once he determined from the reporting witnesses that they believed homicides had taken place, he called the New Jersey State Police.

That basically ended the Coast Guard involvement, though they stayed out there to help protect the integrity of the scene.

I don't ask Lockman any questions. I made my points with Gerdes and have no need to revisit them.

Judge Mahomes adjourns the court for the day. Before the bailiff takes Vogel away, he asks, "How do you think it went?"

"The trial hasn't started yet, Alex."

Big Tony Lynch's body was found propped up against a Laundromat door at Park Avenue and Thirty-third Street. It was discovered by the owner, who as usual arrived at 5:00 A.M. to open the place, fill the vending machines, and make sure the patrons had quarters to access by inserting one-and five-dollar bills.

She screamed when she saw him, and in the early-morning silence the scream echoed through the streets.

Greatly increasing the horror of the scene was that while Tony's body was wedged in the Laundromat doorway, his head was resting against the door of the convenience store next door.

That street corner is just ten blocks from our house on Forty-second Street and Eighteenth Avenue. When Laurie was out for a morning run, she saw the commotion and stopped to see what happened. A cop who she knew from her days on the force told her the details.

She cut her run short to come back to the house, a sure sign that she considers it an important development. If I were out running, I would cut the run short if . . . never mind, it's a hypothetical that is not realistic. I would never be running through the streets; that's why they invented cars.

On her way home she calls Corey and asks him to come right

over. We have to figure out what this development means, other than that the world will have to go on without Big Tony. Corey is here within five minutes after Laurie gets home, and he has Simon in tow, much to Tara's delight.

"This has to be about us," she says, after she tells me what happened.

"I agree. Can't be a coincidence. The question is why, and I can think of two answers."

"Which are?" she prompts.

"The more likely one is that Tony was supposed to kill me the other night and he failed. When Phillips and Bledsoe failed to kill Alex Vogel, their punishment was death, so this is consistent with the pattern.

"The other possibility is that Victor found out that Tony gave us his name and was less than pleased with it."

"How would he have found out?" she asks.

Corey answers, "No way to tell. Could be that Tony told one of his people, or even Russo. Big Tony's brain, even when it was attached to his body, was not the sharpest."

"So you think this is Victor's work, rather than Russo's?" Laurie asks. "Because he also told us that Russo was involved, at least in assigning Tony to work with Victor."

I nod. "The decapitation is not Russo's style; Russo would have had someone put a bullet in Tony's head and leave his body in the park. Or leave it where no one could find it. The boat explosion was not how Russo operates, and this isn't either."

Laurie is nodding as I'm talking. "Absolutely. This was about sending a message. Russo wouldn't have to send anyone a message; he's a known quantity. Victor is a newcomer, so he has to establish fear. People will think twice before they cross him."

"I wonder how Russo feels about this," I say. "He loans out people to Victor, three that we know of, and they all wind up dead. You would think Russo might feel some resentment over that."

"Maybe the message was meant for him."

I nod. "Maybe. If he sits back and takes it, then he's either afraid of Victor and whoever he has brought with him, or he's making enough money that he's willing to suck it up. Either way he must be worried as hell. In a way he has become Victor's employee, and the life expectancy of Victor's employees seems fairly short."

These are all interesting theories, but for our purposes they aren't terribly important. Our focus is not on who actually blew up the boat and killed the two Pharmacon employees; we have no doubt that it was done by Phillips and Bledsoe, under orders from Victor through Big Tony.

"I think Russo is the key. He can lead us to Victor," Corey says.

"How?"

"Physically. I would predict that any past or future meetings between the two of them did not and will not take place at Russo's house. It's a status thing; Victor is the employer here and has the upper hand. He would not want to meet on Russo's turf."

"So?" Laurie prompts.

"So I set up a stakeout. It shouldn't be hard; it's a one-way street out of Russo's house. On the hours I can't be there, maybe Willie can take over."

I shake my head. "Willie can't do it. Russo and his people know him."

"I can sub for you when you can't be there," Laurie says.

I think this is a good idea, except for Laurie's involvement. But I have no chance of winning the argument, and in truth she is smart and knows what she is doing.

"Okay. As long as you guys are careful."

Corey and Laurie look at each other and smile, no doubt amused that I am offering instructions.

"You want to give us some stakeout tips?" Laurie asks.

"Just make sure you have enough doughnuts. Jelly, glazed . . . doesn't really matter."

"Thanks for sharing that," Corey says. Then, "This could work, as long as they have a physical meeting. I know Victor would not give Russo home-field advantage; it's all about the chain of command."

That chain of command has been established in my mind. What I have to find a way to do is get it into the jurors' minds. The initial link of them to our case was Vogel's recognizing Bledsoe's face. I would much rather that he not testify himself, but even if he did, the jury would view his story as self-serving and suspect.

One of the many things I don't understand is why they focused on Vogel. He is not a scientist, and the extent of his knowledge of the new drug was his having papers in his filing cabinet. Why not focus on Giarrusso, the guy who was creating the drug?

Was Giarrusso somehow involved with the conspiracy? Then why kill him? Or was he not supposed to be killed? Could they somehow not have known that Giarrusso was on that boat?

I still don't know how to get to Victor, or even accurately identify him. Maybe he killed Tony, Phillips, and Bledsoe to punish them for their failure, but it also insulates him. We can't get to him through his hired muscle because he has killed them off.

If Giarrusso's new drug is the source of this conspiracy, then we may just have to wait for it to make an impact in the marketplace, or at least in the scientific community.

By then Alex Vogel will be a veteran prisoner.

Patrick Kohler witnessed the explosion out on the ocean.

He made the initial call to the Coast Guard and thereby set in motion a process that ultimately brought him to this courtroom, called to the stand by Trell.

"We were out on my friend Bobby Simmons's boat. It was the four of us, Bobby and his wife, Arlene, and me and my wife, Callie. We had left port the day before and were heading back that afternoon."

"And at some point you came into contact with the defendant's boat, the *Doral*?"

"We saw them, yes. We got within maybe a hundred yards. Close enough to wave."

"Did they wave back?"

"Actually, no. We didn't really see any movement on the deck. We thought we saw a man sunbathing."

"What did you do next?"

"We got a little closer and Callie commented that the man looked strange; he was lying at an unusual angle. He was wedged up against a bench, and one arm was draped over him. It just didn't look right. So someone, I think it was Bobby, went to get a pair of binoculars that he had below. He came up and handed them to me."

"And you trained it on the *Doral?*"

"Yes. I saw the man on the deck. He was wearing a shirt and it was covered in something dark; I believed then and I believe now that it was blood. As I was handing the binoculars to Bobby to take a look, there was this huge explosion. I mean, the boat was there, and then it wasn't. We felt a huge impact. I thought we were going to tip over."

"Is that when you called the Coast Guard?"

"It is."

Once again I am handed a witness who cannot effectively be challenged because he is telling the truth and clearly has no ax to grind. So all I can do is ask a few mild questions and get out.

"Mr. Kohler, you say you only saw one person?"

"Correct."

"And you believed he was at least unconscious and also was covered in blood?"

"That's what it looked like to me. But I can't be sure, of course."

"Were there any other boats in the area?"

"Not directly there, but it was a beautiful day. There were boats in the distance."

"You could see them?"

"Yes."

"About how far away was the closest one? I know it's difficult to be precise; your best guess is what I'm looking for."

He thinks for a few moments. "Maybe two and a half nautical miles."

"How fast can a boat cover that distance?"

He shrugs. "Depends on the boat."

"Say a boat like yours, just as an example."

"At full speed, maybe fifteen minutes."

"So it is conceivable that a boat you saw in the distance could have been adjacent to the *Doral* fifteen minutes earlier?"

"I suppose so, yes."

"You would have no way of knowing if that happened either way, right?"

"Right."

"And if someone from that boat in the distance had actually been aboard the *Doral,* twenty or thirty minutes earlier, you wouldn't have any way of knowing that either, would you?"

"That's correct."

"So you only have knowledge of what was on the deck of the *Doral* when you approached it. You couldn't know what happened before then. Correct?"

"Correct."

"Thank you. No further questions."

Next on Trell's hit parade is Arlene Blouch. She was at the pier the day that Vogel, Mellman, and Giarrusso set sail on their ill-fated trip.

"Why were you at the pier that day?"

"We were going out on our boat, my husband and I. Ours docks right next to where Alex's . . . Mr. Vogel's . . . was docked."

"Did you see him there often?"

"Yes, almost every weekend in the spring and summer."

"Would you describe yourself as friends?"

"Yes, I would. I mean we didn't go out socially or anything, but we had spent some time on each other's boats. I would say that my husband and I considered him a friend, yes."

"So you couldn't mistake him for someone else, or someone else for him?" Trell asks.

"Definitely not."

"Please describe what happened when you saw Alex Vogel that day."

"Well, we got there a little late; usually we go out before he does. But he was already there, and I saw him getting on his boat with two other men. I called and waved to him, but he didn't respond. I can't be sure that he heard me."

"Were they talking to each other?"

"Yes, they were arguing, or at least that's what it seemed like. I couldn't make out most of what they were saying, and it wasn't any of my business, but I clearly heard one of them say, 'Come on, that's a bunch of crap.' He sounded angry."

Arlene Blouch has done two things for Trell. She's placed Vogel on the boat that day with Mellman and Giarrusso. Trell considers that important, but I don't, since we were not planning to contest it.

Blouch has also introduced that the men were arguing. That is more damaging to us; it doesn't quite create a motive, but it's something the jury will certainly consider. That's the main, but not the only, area for me to focus on in my cross-examination of her.

"Ms. Blouch, was Alex Vogel carrying anything when he boarded the boat that day?"

"I don't believe so."

"Other than the fact that you heard what you thought was arguing, nothing seemed out of the ordinary? Everybody seemed to be boarding voluntarily?"

"Yes."

"No one was at gunpoint?" I ask.

"No."

"The phrase 'Come on, that's a bunch of crap' . . . who said that?"

"I don't know."

"Was it Alex Vogel?"

"No, it was one of the other two men. Definitely not Alex's voice."

"So there were three people, let's call them A, B, and C. If Alex is A, could C have been yelling at B?"

"It's possible."

"So Alex might not have been involved in the conversation at all?"

"I guess that's true."

"When you heard this argument, were you worried?"

"About what?"

"Maybe that it might break into violence?"

"No, it wasn't that bad. I only mentioned it to the police because of what happened."

"So when you heard it, you didn't consider calling the police at that point?"

"Not even close."

"You said you considered Alex a friend."

"Yes."

"You found him pleasant, polite, enjoyable to be around?"

"Yes. He was especially nice to my children. I appreciated that. And he often had his dog with him; he loves that dog."

"Any hint of violence, ever?"

"None."

"Thank you."

Today starts the parade of witnesses that can seriously damage us.

Until now Trell has been building the foundation with witnesses that could not be challenged because not only were they telling a simple truth, but we were fine with what they were saying.

That's about to change.

The first witness up today is Sergeant Troy Willeford. He's in charge of forensics for the division of the New Jersey State Police that covers Long Beach Island. He was on the scene of the explosion that day and supervised the forensics of the entire case.

Once Trell establishes both Willeford's credentials and that he was out on the ocean that day, Trell asks, "Were you able to recover any of the wreckage?"

"Yes, nothing was intact, but there were certainly pieces floating around. We got there quickly, so were lucky to get what we got."

"Were you able to find anything significant?"

"Yes, I believe so. We found traces of Cintron 421."

"What is that?"

"An extraordinarily powerful explosive. Military grade."

"Had you encountered it in your work before?"

"Yes, but rarely. It's very volatile and takes a real expertise to handle."

Trell feigns surprise. "Military grade? So a serviceman trained in munitions might typically be expected to be familiar with it?"

"Most would, yes."

"Have you encountered Cintron 421 since that day on the ocean?"

"Yes, when we executed a search warrant on Mr. Vogel's house. There were traces of it on his worktable."

Trell gives that a moment to sink in. "He was working with Cintron 421 in his house?"

"I can't be sure of that. All I can say with certainty is that there were traces of it on the worktable."

"Did you find anything else in the boat wreckage?"

"Blood traces. DNA determined that it belonged to Mr. Giarrusso."

Trell asks him a few more questions, mostly to get him to repeat the incriminating things he's already said, then turns him over to me.

"Sergeant Willeford, you talked about Cintron 421 being volatile."

"Yes."

"What do you mean by that?"

"Well, it is more prone than most explosives to detonate accidentally."

"How might that happen?"

"Well, depending on how it is stored, or the device it is housed in, perhaps it could be powerfully shaken, maybe exposed to intense heat. . . ."

"Did any of those things happen on the *Doral*?"

"I couldn't say."

"So it might have gone off accidentally? Is that possible?"

"I wasn't there."

"That would be a good answer if my question had been 'Sergeant Willeford, were you there?' But I asked if it was possible for it to have gone off accidentally."

"Yes, that's possible. I don't have enough information to determine if it did or not."

"Thank you. Now regarding soldiers with munitions training. If you know, do they go to a lab or workroom and physically mix chemicals or materials to make explosives?"

"No, I wouldn't think so. The munitions come to them fully prepared. They are manufactured in factories."

"You said that you found traces of Cintron 421 in Mr. Vogel's house, is that correct?"

"Yes."

"Any other bomb-making equipment?"

"No."

"If you know, who put those traces there?"

"I don't know."

"Are you aware that Mr. Vogel's house was broken into the day after the explosion on the *Doral*, before you guys inspected it?"

"Yes, it was quite obvious that the house had been ransacked."

"Could the person or persons who broke in have left the Cintron 421 traces?"

"I don't know."

"You don't know if it's possible?"

"I suppose it's possible."

"Can you say beyond a reasonable doubt that it didn't happen that way?"

"I cannot, no."

"Thank you, no further questions."

Pharmacon CEO Eric Buckner called the meeting to discuss a crucial matter.

In the wake of events in Cumberland, New York, a significant decision had to be made.

Ruth and Glenn Radford, having contracted an infection caused by *Diveria aureus,* had been cured by Loraxil. Since Pharmacon's survival most likely depended on Loraxil's success, the importance of this event could not be overstated.

Pharmacon had sent two scientists to Cumberland to confer and consult with scientists from the CDC and FDA. All parties agreed that the Radfords in fact had the ailment, and that their recovery after receiving Loraxil was stunning.

Most significant, the government entities believed that the drug could likely attack other so-called superbugs.

Reflecting the importance of this meeting now, it was attended by only three people, none of whom brought any staff along. In addition to Buckner, there was CFO Gerald Bennings and Chief Scientist Jordan Tucker.

Alex Vogel would have been the fourth attendee, but he could not be there for obvious reasons. Since he had not yet been replaced, Bennings had taken over his responsibilities for the time being.

Bennings started by giving an update on where things stood with the FDA, independent of the events in Cumberland. "We've got all of our testing data over there. It's impressive, and we should get approval on the merits. The problem, as you know, is that it is limited in scope. We do not and cannot have many case results because there have been so few cases reported. So mostly it has been animal testing, and the data is very impressive."

"This changes things dramatically," Buckner said. "Does it not?"

"It does, but things still move slowly in the bureaucracy. The FDA people will go back and tell their bosses what happened, and it will be given consideration. I am told, though, that it is unlikely it will be fast-tracked."

"Not even after Cumberland?" Tucker asked.

Bennings shook his head. "Correct. They will not see this as a public emergency; to them it is a one-off. And they probably are correct."

"So Cumberland makes our case more compelling but still doesn't carry the day?" Buckner asked. "Is that what you're telling me?"

"That's my view," Bennings said.

"What if there was a breakout of the disease? If there was a cluster and a bunch of people contracted it? Do we have the supply to deal with it if called upon to do so?"

That was Tucker's area, and he answered quickly, "No, absolutely not. We barely had enough to deal with Cumberland. We are producing it on a need basis, and that need has not been there so far. We could mass-produce, but it's expensive. Still, I think we should do it."

Bennings was shaking his head before Tucker even finished. "Way too expensive; it's just not practical at this point. Not without government approval and financial incentives. If we go ahead, and the FDA doesn't sign off on it soon, we're history."

Nothing more was to be said. Buckner agreed with Bennings, so they would not start mass production. All they could do was wait.

Cumberland was a huge plus for Pharmacon's prospects, but they remained prospects. For the time being Loraxil would remain in limbo, and so would the company.

Now that Trell has placed Vogel on the boat, he needs to get him off it.

All the jury knows, at least from the testimony at trial, is that he boarded the *Doral* with two other men and that it blew up. Since they can see Alex Vogel at the defense table, they know he escaped, but they don't know how.

Telling them is Trell's job today.

He calls Lieutenant Susan Kelly of the Long Beach Township Police Department to accomplish it. Her job will not be difficult.

"Lieutenant Kelly, were you called to the home of a Mr. Walter Ambrose the day after the explosion on the *Doral*?"

"The call came in to our department. I answered it."

"That home is in a town called Loveladies, which is on Long Beach Island?"

She nods. "That's correct."

Trell introduces as evidence a large map of Long Beach Island, and he uses it to demonstrate how Loveladies is almost at the opposite end of the island from Beach Haven, where the *Doral* had been docked. He makes it sound like suspicious behavior, which it is.

Then, "Why had Mr. Ambrose called your department?"

"A dinghy had come onshore at his private dock. He did not

see it when it arrived, so did not know who had been on it. But it was concerning to him, so he contacted us."

"And you found it?"

"We did; Mr. Ambrose directed us to it."

"Did you determine who it belonged to?"

She nods. "Yes, there was identification on the side which indicated it was attached to the *Doral,* Mr. Vogel's boat."

"By then you had known about the boat explosion?"

"Of course."

"Did you know at that point who had been on the dinghy?"

"No."

Trell gets Lieutenant Kelly to say that she learned that Vogel rented a car from a rental-car agency across the causeway, therefore off the island.

"Is there a rental-car agency on the island?"

"Yes."

"But he chose not to use it?"

"I can't speak to any choice he might have made; I can only tell you which place he used and which he didn't."

"Was his own car still parked at the Beach Haven pier?"

"It was."

"Did Mr. Vogel report to your department what had happened out on the water?"

"He did not."

On cross-examination I cannot once again successfully challenge any of the facts, since they are all completely accurate. Vogel did use the dinghy to land in Loveladies, he did leave his car in Beach Haven, and he failed to report to police.

His claim is that he was afraid his pursuers might somehow know he was alive and might be searching for him, so he wanted to escape as quickly and cleanly as possible. But he's not on the stand, so I have no way to get that across.

"Lieutenant Kelly, if Mr. Vogel intentionally sailed that dinghy to Loveladies rather than Beach Haven, do you know why?"

"I can only speculate."

"Is it possible he misjudged where he was coming in? Was there any navigation equipment on the dinghy?"

"I can't say what his intentions were. No, there was no navigation equipment on there."

"You said before that you could speculate on why he acted the way he did. Would part of that speculation be that he wanted to escape detection, to hide?"

"Definitely, yes."

"In your experience, is one of the reasons that people hide to escape danger?"

"Yes."

"Sometimes they see that danger as coming from the police. Correct?"

"Yes."

"Might that danger also come from someone else? For example, if the average person believed that hired killers had murdered two friends and had that person next on their list, might that person also have reason to hide?"

"It's possible."

"Fear of murder is only a 'possible' reason to hide?"

"It depends on the person."

"You mean, you've met people who when threatened with death adopt the 'Come and get me too, Chino' approach?'" I'm not sure how many jurors will get the *West Side Story* reference, but it is understandable in any event. Most of the jurors smile, so I think they get it.

"Here's a hypothetical. Please answer based on your experience and common sense. If an average person, having never been involved in violence in his life, saw two friends murdered, barely escaped his own death, and believed the killers were still after him . . . would that person have reason to be afraid? And could the stress of that situation possibly cause him to make rash decisions?"

Trell objects and Mahomes makes me withdraw the question on the grounds that I am testifying, rather than cross-examining. It's a fair point, but I've already made my own point, so I let her off the stand.

Andy, I know this is not going well."

Alex had asked to speak to me for ten minutes before the afternoon session starts, so we're meeting in an anteroom. He's obviously down and worried about our prospects.

"Have you been speaking to Hike?" I ask.

Alex smiles. "As rarely as possible. But it has nothing to do with Hike. I'm not stupid, contrary to what my actions in this case would indicate. I can tell that the prosecution is holding all the cards. I just wanted to thank you and tell you I appreciate everything; no one could do it better."

"We've got a long way to go," I say, mainly because we do have a long way to go.

"I know, and I hope I'm wrong, but there's one other thing. . . ."

"What's that?"

"Promise me you'll find a good home for Aggie. I can't tell you how much I love that dog."

"There are very few promises I can make to my clients, Alex . . . other than I will try my best. But this is one I can make: no matter what, Aggie will be with people who love her."

"Thank you."

The bailiff comes in to tell us that court is coming back into session.

As Alex gets up, I touch his arm to stop him. "One more thing, Alex. Stop talking to Hike."

"I never do. Hike talks to me."

Trell's final witness today is probably the one that will wrap up his case. He is Captain William Shenton of the New Jersey State Police, Homicide Division, and he was the chief investigator on this case. He is also the cop that arrested Alex Vogel.

"Captain Shenton, this was your case, is that correct?" Trell asks.

"I led the investigative team, yes."

"When you initially were brought in, did you think Alex Vogel died in the explosion?"

"I had no reason to believe otherwise. We had a strong indication that he had been on board, and there was no evidence of any survivors."

"How long were you into the investigation when you came to consider it a homicide?"

"Very early on."

"Why was that? What made you come to that determination?"

"Two things. One was the interview with the people on the other boat. They said that they believed there was a body covered in blood before the explosion even took place. So that was compelling. But then the fact that Cintron 421 was used; that just doesn't happen to be stored on a pleasure boat. It had to be brought there for a reason. At least that was our reasoning."

"Did you have a suspect?"

"Not at that point, because there were two possibilities. It was either a triple homicide, or a murder/suicide. It was plausible that one of the people on the boat deliberately took their own life as well as the others."

"When did that change?"

"When we found the dinghy. That didn't get to the pier in Loveladies by itself. It was clear that one of the people from that boat had gotten away. Then when we got the rental-car information, we were certain that Mr. Vogel had survived."

"So he became a suspect?"

"Yes, we believed, and I believed, that not coming to the police and not coming forward when the media widely reported him dead showed what we call a consciousness of guilt. It wasn't yet proof, but the discovery of traces of Cintron 421 in his house made his guilt, in my mind, a certainty. The fact that he was in munitions in the army cemented it even further."

Trell questions Shenton for a while longer, mostly to reaffirm what he has already said, rather than to extract new information. He does get Shenton to say that he believes that the bomb was detonated remotely rather than set on a timer, but he has no forensic information that supports this. Bottom line is that it does not matter.

I start my cross by asking if he checked out other boats in the area near the explosion.

"We put out word that we would like to speak to anyone out there who had any information."

"So you didn't send boats out yourself to find and interview people?"

"No. They would have been too dispersed by the time we could have done that."

"So if someone on another boat had committed this crime, by putting out word that people with information should come forward, you were hoping they would show up and confess? You were operating on the honor system?"

I can tell by the look on his face that he's pissed. "That was not our hope or expectation, no."

"Is it your theory that Mr. Vogel set off the explosion to kill his friends in the way he did as part of a plan to fake his own death?"

"That is my theory, yes. But the why is not as important as the facts."

"So when the facts are created by people, you don't generally find that there is a reason for doing what they did?"

"There is always a reason, sometimes rational, sometimes not."

I nod and walk back to the defense table so Hike can hand me a piece of paper. As I do, so I see that Laurie has entered the back of the courtroom. We make eye contact, but I can't figure out why she's here. There must be a reason; she sure as hell wasn't just in the neighborhood.

I introduce the paper as evidence, and I give copies to Trell and the witness, as well as Judge Mahomes. "Captain Shenton, can you describe this document for the jury?"

"It's a rental form for dock space at the pier in Long Beach Island. It's for the *Doral,* and it has been signed and paid for by Mr. Vogel."

"Is it dated the same date as the explosion?"

"Yes."

"And does it cover rental for the month before or after that date?"

"After."

"Does it seem strange to you that Mr. Vogel paid in advance for a month's boat rental when he was planning to destroy that boat and disappear two hours later?"

"Perhaps he was trying to get people to think exactly what you are implying now."

"Why would he care what people thought about his boat rental when his plan was for them to think he was dead?"

"I couldn't say."

"I'm sure you couldn't."

Trell objects that I'm badgering, and Mahomes sustains.

"Captain Shenton, had you ever seen this piece of paper before today?"

"Yes."

"But you didn't think it was worth disclosing it to this jury?"

"I don't consider it important or particularly relevant, no."

"Do you consider Mr. Vogel's actions well thought out? All planned in advance?"

"Yes."

"So signing for a rental car with his own identification was part of his planning?"

"It wasn't a perfect plan, obviously."

"How did you come to find him?"

"The Paterson police notified us that they had a tip that he had come forward under an assumed name to retrieve his dog."

"Why would he do that?"

"He was apparently attached to the dog," Shenton says, frowning.

"That is admirable. But if he was so attached to his dog, why wouldn't he have made arrangements to keep the dog in a place where he could get her without having to reveal himself? What kind of plan is that?"

"Plans aren't always perfect."

"Neither are theories. That's why they need to be challenged."

I let Shenton off and Mahomes adjourns court for the day. I say a quick good-bye to Vogel and head for the back of the courtroom to talk to Laurie.

"What's going on?"

"Corey called; Junior's on the move."

We head home to await developments.

Corey had called to say that Joseph Russo, Jr., had left his house and gotten in a car with three bodyguards. Corey followed them to a warehouse in Glen Rock. They went in about forty-five minutes ago, and we're waiting anxiously for Corey's next report.

He calls five minutes after we get home, and Laurie puts it on speakerphone. "Russo and his people left two minutes ago. I decided not to follow them. I want to see who comes out of the warehouse next."

"Smart," Laurie says. "We know where Russo will be whenever we want to get back on him."

"Maybe we won't have to," I say.

"Somebody's coming out," Corey says. "Call you later."

Later turns out to be twenty-five minutes. "I think we have Victor." The excitement is evident in Corey's voice.

"Where are you?"

"I followed him to a motel in Garfield. It's just off the highway and it's one of those places where you can drive around to your room and enter from the outside."

"What makes you think it's him?"

"Just the fact that Russo went to him. He's also a big guy

and has an Eastern European look about him, whatever that is. Bottom line is that I don't know for sure, but I'd bet I'm right."

"Were you able to get a picture?"

"No, tried but never really had a chance. The good news is that it's a big parking lot with a good view of his room. We can easily watch him undetected."

"What's the name of the motel and room number?" I ask. "Maybe Sam can find out who is in that room."

"It's called the Senator Motor Inn and he's in room 208. I'll get his license number also and call it in."

"Great," Laurie says. "I would say you should give it twenty minutes or so, and if he doesn't leave, come back here and we'll figure out our next steps."

"Will do."

I call Sam and give him the hotel name and room information. "Piece of cake," he says. Then Corey calls and gives us the license plate number on the car. When I call back and relay that to Sam he says, "Piece of cake."

Corey gets to the house about forty-five minutes later. He's starving, having not had a chance to eat all day except for some pretzels he had in the car. Laurie heats up some leftover chicken parmigiana from last night, and he inhales it as he talks.

"What do you guys think?" he asks.

"I see two choices," Laurie says. "One is we go to the police and tell them who we believe he is. Two is we watch him, see what he does, and hopefully get some insight as to what is going on."

I shake my head. "There is no choice to be made. Number two is our only option."

"Why?" Corey asks. He and Laurie, as ex-cops, usually lean toward bringing them in.

"Because our job is not to cleanse the world of bad guys. Our job is to defend our client. If the FBI comes in and takes Victor off to prison, or turns him over to Interpol, or even just alerts him that we know about him, then we gain nothing and our client loses everything."

"I agree with Andy," Corey says.

That is shocking news. "You agree with me? Are we in an alternate universe?"

He smiles. "It wasn't easy to get those words out, believe me. But I see no obligation to bring the police in. First of all, we don't even know who it is, and we may not know for a while. I doubt Sam is going to find out he checked into the hotel using the name Victor and listing his occupation as Russian Mafia guy.

"Second, we have absolutely no information that he is wanted for a crime, here or anywhere. And we obviously have no independent proof that he's done anything that we could give the cops."

I nod. "I would like to associate myself with everything Corey just said."

"Even I can't argue with it," Laurie says.

The phone rings and it's Sam. "The motel room and the rental car are both in the name of Luther Walker. The driver's license he gave to get the car is bogus, so it's pretty safe to assume that Luther Walker is not Luther Walker. No way to know who it is, unless you can get a fingerprint."

We thank Sam and hang up. Corey immediately says, "I don't think fingerprints are practical at this point. His car is out in the open within easy sight of his window. Also, if we tried to get into it, we would have to hurry and might leave traces which he could detect. Getting into the room on a ruse, or breaking in when he leaves, also seems way too risky."

Laurie nods her agreement, and I say, "At this point it's not crucial that we even know his identity, whether his name is

Victor or something else. It's more important that we know what he's done and what he's doing from this point."

"So we maintain surveillance," Corey says. "I'll take most of it, but I would think Willie and even Sam could help."

I shake my head. "Sam might go in shooting. What about Marcus?"

"I think Marcus should be a backup," Laurie says. "He can be called in at any time if Victor starts to move."

I'm not sure I agree with that, but Laurie and Corey know more than I do about this kind of stuff. And with the defense case, or at least what there is of it, about to begin, I'm going to have to leave it in their hands. "Whatever you guys say."

"I'll call Willie," Laurie says.

Figuring out the money connection to this case is frustrating me.

Whatever is going on has to be about money; it can't be anything else. It sure as hell is not about Russo junior being jealous about Carla D'Antoni dating Alex Vogel.

Russo has turned over some of his people, literally sacrificed those people, because the man we know as Victor has enough money to solve Russo's somewhat desperate financial situation. For whatever cash infusion that represents, it's certainly not a few thousand bucks. It has to be big-time money.

But so far I've been thinking about this from everyone's point of view other than Victor's. If Victor is calling the shots, then his motivation, or the motivation of those he represents, is what is important. What is *he* getting out of it?

The answer has to be money, but that answer is counterintuitive. How could Victor need money if he's buying his way into this in the first place? His resources are substantial enough to be buying Russo, so he can't exactly be starving.

Why would the Russian Mafia, represented by Victor, be here in the first place if not for money? I can't think of a reason, yet if there is one thing they have demonstrated, it's that they already have plenty of money.

I can think of two possibilities. One goes back to something that Robby Divine had said to me when we talked about the Pharmacon IPO, something that is sticking in my mind. He implied, admittedly without evidence, that some of the money investors were putting up might be dirty. Money in need of laundering sounds like an organized crime type of doing business.

But there are two problems with that. One is that I don't see why Russian organized crime would need to launder their money here. Lieutenant Guttierez, an expert in this area, said that they are already sharing their wealth with members of the Russian government. With that kind of protection in place, I would think that they could operate with relative impunity and not have to launder money.

The other problem is that if the goal was simply to launder money, then hasn't it already been accomplished? They bought their stock; why don't they just sell it and move on?

Based on what I know, it defies logic. On the other hand, what do I know? I place a call to Sam Willis to ask if he can find out who invested in Pharmacon.

"Do they release the information?" I ask.

"They don't have to go out of their way to release it. Unless it's of an amount or the type of purchaser that can influence future trading?"

"What kind of purchaser would that be?"

"Obvious example would be Warren Buffett, but it might be influential hedge funds, that kind of thing. But not to worry, stock purchases are ultimately public information. Either way, I'll find it. What are you looking for?"

"Help."

Laurie comes into the office to offer me coffee, and I tell her my thinking on all of this, including the second possibility:

that so much money is involved, then what Victor is putting up to buy Russo is a drop in the bucket.

"Or Russo is in on it," she says. "Maybe he isn't just getting paid by Victor for the use of his men, but instead has a piece of whatever it is that Victor is doing. Maybe he's getting a percentage."

"That makes sense. More than the money-laundering angle. But where is the windfall coming from? Giarrusso's new drug idea? Is the Russian Mafia betting on entering the pharmaceutical business?"

"Have we heard any indication that whoever stole it has been trying to develop it?"

I shake my head. "I haven't. Both Bennings and Tucker, the finance and science guys at Pharmacon, told me they would notify me if they heard anything. Of course, they could have just been saying that to get me out of their offices."

"But the bad guys did steal that drug information from the filing cabinet at Vogel's house. That is a fact."

"Right. So they tried to kill the three people that were forming a company to develop that drug. They got two, but missed Vogel. Could it be that simple?"

"Vogel said he was the target," she says.

"And Big Tony said the same thing. Maybe they were wrong. Maybe Tony misspoke; he wasn't the brightest, and Marcus had just used him as a discus. And maybe Vogel misheard what was said on the boat; he was in fear for his life. Maybe Vogel was just one of the targets."

"We're working with a lot of maybes."

Yes, we are.

O

ne thing has not changed since the beginning of this case:

Our only chance for success rests with our being able to convince the jury of the possibility that someone else could have done it. We always knew that we were going to have to point to someone and say to the jury, *Look at that guy . . . maybe it was him.*

We were never going to be able to point to Alex Vogel and say that it couldn't possibly have been him. The facts simply would not make that credible.

So we're left with Russo and Company.

The courtroom has been crowded every day of the trial; I wouldn't say it qualifies as a huge story, but there has been a good amount of public interest. The media coverage has been substantial as well; I've turned down a bunch of offers to do interviews.

My approach to dealing with the media is simple. If it helps my client, I do it. If it doesn't, I don't. It's fairly easy to make those judgments, so I rarely have to struggle with those decisions.

In our defense opening I am going to refer to a different, earlier media story, and to do it, I'm calling in a favor. Actually, more than one.

Vince Sanders is my first witness. He hates appearing in public and also doesn't think as a journalist he should be seen as taking sides. But he hates buying his own beer and burgers even more. He also knows I am pissed at him for running that story about Alex Vogel coming forward to get Aggie, one that I believe sped up his arrest.

So Vince has reluctantly agreed to testify and trudges to the stand as if he is pulling a heavy wagon. I could have used anyone for this job; I'm using Vince both because he has some stature in the community, and because I want to get revenge on his ass.

I take him through his credentials as a leading member of the media and current editor of the local paper. Then I ask, "Does the name Carla D'Antoni mean anything to you?"

"Yes, she was a young woman that unfortunately became a murder victim earlier this year. She was thrown off of a warehouse building in downtown Paterson."

"Did you run a story about it?"

"Of course we did."

I introduce a newspaper article as evidence and show it to him. "Is this your story?"

"Yes."

"Did I ask you to research whether it was widely covered in print and television?"

"You did, and it was."

I get him to read the section where it mentions that Carla D'Antoni was rumored to be the girlfriend of Joseph Russo, Jr. I don't have to go into detail about who Russo is; the jury would know, and the article makes a veiled reference to his underworld connections.

Next I show Vince a more recent article, also in his paper, which mentions that Vogel also dated Carla D'Antoni. "Was this also widely covered?"

"It was."

"Do you think dating Joseph Russo, Jr.'s girlfriend is a good idea?"

"I don't." Vince says the words before Trell can object, but once he does, Mahomes tells the court reporter to strike it from the record.

"Let me ask it another way. Do you think it is a good idea for Joseph Russo's girlfriend to be caught dating someone else?"

This time Trell is out of his chair like it is an ejector seat, and Mahomes doesn't just admonish me, he warns me to be careful. That's okay, I've made my point.

I turn Vince over to Trell, and he walks to the podium shaking his head, as if irritated he has to deal with this nonsense.

"Mr. Sanders, do you have any knowledge as to who killed Carla D'Antoni?"

"No."

"To your knowledge, have the police made any arrests?"

"I don't believe so, no."

"Do you have any knowledge as to whether Mr. Russo knew that Mr. Vogel and Carla D'Antoni had dated?"

"I do not."

"Thank you, no further questions."

My next move is to recall New Jersey State Police sergeant Troy Willeford, the forensic cop who testified in the prosecution's case.

"Sergeant, you testified that there was a break-in at Alex Vogel's house the day after the boat explosion. Is that correct?"

"We believe so, although we cannot be sure exactly when the robbery took place."

"You called it a robbery. What was stolen?"

"That is unclear because we have no way of knowing what was in the house before the event."

"So it's possible nothing was taken?"

"It's possible."

"And it's possible the purpose of the break-in was in fact to leave incriminating evidence behind."

"Anything is possible" is Willeford's grudging admission. We had gone over this in cross-examination, but there's no downside in beating it into the jury's probably bored heads.

I show Willeford police photographs of the inside of Vogel's house, obviously taken after the robbery. One of them shows the inside of the closet, without no filing cabinet to be seen. He confirms that they are in fact police photos.

Next I show him a Facebook photograph Vogel posted of Aggie a couple of months ago. Behind her can be seen the open closet, with the filing cabinet very much there.

"Sergeant, do you know what happened to that filing cabinet?"

"I do not."

Later I am going to use the missing filing cabinet to introduce information about Robert Giarrusso's Alzheimer's drug.

I let Willeford off the stand, having once again challenged the forensic discovery of Cintron 421 in the house. If Vogel is going to testify in his own defense, and I am leaning in that direction, then the trace explosives is the only thing he cannot explain away.

All he could offer would be what would appear to be a self-serving denial. I am going to ask that Vogel be brought to court early tomorrow, so that we can start to discuss the possibility of his testifying.

During the break I retrieve a phone message from Laurie, who tells me that Corey reports that Victor is on the move. Nothing special yet, just out to a diner to eat.

Corey is going to try to get a photograph of his face, but so far the opportunity has not presented itself. I have mixed feelings about that.

If we identify him from a photograph, then find out that he is wanted for any felonies, we would have a legal obligation to report it. I don't generally worry about legal obligations; I find them pretty annoying. But Laurie and Corey feel differently about them.

I can just add it to the list of things to worry about.

Next I call Pete Stanton, who is even less comfortable help-ing the defense than Vince Sanders.

Too bad, Pete. I'm thinking. *You and Vince are finding out that when it comes to beer and burgers, there's no such thing as a free lunch.*

Unlike Vince, who merely served as a conduit to report on media coverage, Pete has firsthand information that is directly related to our case.

"Captain Stanton, please relate the circumstances in which you first met Mr. Vogel."

"It was at your dog rescue foundation. You had alerted me that he was going to be there at that time."

"Did I say why?"

"Yes, you said that you had his dog and that he wanted her back. Knowing he was missing and presumed dead, you thought it might be something I would be interested in."

"And he did show up as predicted?"

"He did."

"When you introduced yourself, did he make any effort to run away?"

Pete shakes his head. "No, but he also wouldn't come down to the station to answer questions."

"As was his right?"

Pete nods. "As was his right as explained to him by you. Even though you said you were not yet his attorney." It's a minor dig at me, but not significant.

"Are you familiar with the names Charles Phillips and Orlando Bledsoe?"

"Yes. Both of those men were victims of homicides on the same night. They were shot to death."

"In what would commonly be known as execution-style?"

"Yes."

"Have you made any arrests in that case?"

"Not yet."

"And this took place after the boat explosion? Is that correct?"

"Yes. Weeks after."

"And just a few days after it was reported in the media that Mr. Vogel was alive?"

"That's correct."

"Is it your understanding that the late Mr. Phillips and Mr. Bledsoe had a relationship with Joseph Russo, Jr.?"

"Yes, they were employed by him. I'm not sure what the status was at the time of their death."

Trell interrupts and asks the judge for a bench conference, and Judge Mahomes tells us to approach.

"Judge, we are very far afield here. This is a fishing expedition that has little or no relevance to our case."

"It's about to become very relevant, Your Honor, despite Mr. Trell's attempt to avoid it."

We argue some more, after which the judge allows me to continue. "But you better demonstrate that relevance soon, Mr. Carpenter."

"Yes, Your Honor."

I introduce as evidence a document and ask Pete to describe

it. "It appears to be a boat-charter receipt from a company in . . . Toms River, New Jersey."

"And who is listed as the person chartering the boat?"

"Orlando Bledsoe."

"The same Orlando Bledsoe who worked for Joseph Russo?"

"I couldn't say."

I hand Pete the other document, which is a copy of the scanned driver's license that Bledsoe had to provide to the charter company. "Now, let me ask you again. Is that the same Orlando Bledsoe that worked for Joseph Russo?"

"It looks like him, yes."

"How far is it from Toms River to the location on the ocean where the explosion happened?"

"I couldn't say."

"If I told you that it was slightly over fifteen nautical miles, would you have any reason to doubt that?"

"No."

Next I introduce more documents and ask him to examine them and tell the jury what they are. Two are receipts for burner phones purchased by Bledsoe at the electronics store, bought with Bledsoe's credit card.

Next I introduce GPS records from the phones that we have subpoenaed from the cell phone provider. We already knew what they would say, courtesy of Sam, but we needed to get them this way so that we could legally introduce them into the trial record.

I get Pete to say that the records show the phones were in Toms River at the time of the boat charter. We don't need it to prove the charter; Bledsoe's credit card records and the charter document itself did that. But this adds further proof that it was Bledsoe's phone.

I direct Pete to a different place on the document, one that shows that Bledsoe's phone was at the warehouse address at the time that Carla D'Antoni was pushed off the building.

I can see that he is stunned to see this. "You should have come to us with this," he says, admonishing me.

"We received it two days ago." It's technically the truth, since that's when we received the legal version.

"Then you should have come to us two days ago."

"You needed this information urgently? Did you want to make a quick arrest because you consider these two dead men a flight risk?"

Judge Mahomes rather forcefully tells us to stop arguing, and I'm fine with that. I've gotten what I wanted and made Pete look bad.

It's a win-win.

When I get home, there's a message from Carla D'Antoni's sister, Linda. I call her back immediately in the hope that she's learned something that might help and is not just wanting me to tell her if I've made progress finding her sister's killer.

"I finally got up the nerve to go through Carla's things. I don't think I found anything, but there is something I wanted to ask you about. Some advice, really."

"Happy to help if I can."

"In her things, actually hidden in a drawer, was nine thousand dollars in cash. Hundred-dollar bills."

I'm not terribly surprised to hear this; Sam had learned that she made three $9,000 cash deposits, one each week. I can only assume that this was meant to be deposit number four.

"What did you want to ask me?"

"Well, in addition to this, she had almost thirty thousand dollars in the bank, and she left it to me. What should I do with it?"

"I don't understand, Linda. You're asking me how you should spend your money?"

"It's not my money, it's Carla's."

"Now it's yours."

"I know, but . . . I don't know how she got it. What if she did something wrong?"

"It's in the past, Linda. I imagine that Carla would want you to enjoy the money, to do things that are important to you and help you live your life."

"You're probably right, but it doesn't feel great." Then Linda laughs a short laugh, but not the kind you laugh when you think something is funny. "Too bad she never gave me the stock tips she promised."

"You and me both. Linda, don't agonize over this. She wouldn't want you to."

"I lost my sister. I still can't believe it."

Corey and Willie set up a schedule to watch and follow Victor.

Because of our limited manpower, nothing close to 24-7 coverage was possible. We decided that the chance of his doing something was more significant in the evening and night hours, so Willie took from ten in the morning until four in the afternoon.

After that it would be Corey, until whatever time seemed appropriate. If Victor was in his hotel at 10:00 P.M. with the lights out, for example, Corey would feel that it was okay to leave.

On this day Victor left the motel at 7:00 P.M. Corey assumed Victor was going to dinner, but instead he drove up the Palisades Interstate Parkway, finally getting off at the exit north of Pomona, New York.

With little automobile traffic, Corey stayed a longer-than-usual distance behind Victor. It would be better to lose him than to be discovered following him, but fortunately Corey remained in contact.

Victor ultimately drove to a rural, hilly area. At the bottom of a small road that went almost a quarter mile up a hill was a sign for the Jefferson Home for Seniors. He went up the hill, but Corey could not follow him without its being completely obvious to Victor that he was under surveillance.

Corey got as close as he safely could and took out his binoculars. It was getting dark and hard to see. Corey could see a large building at the top of the hill and what looked like a small shed about three-quarters of the way up.

Halfway up the hill, Victor turned the lights off on his own car. Corey had no idea why, but assumed that Victor did not to want to be seen.

He thought that Victor stopped near the shed, but in the dark it was hard to tell for sure. Corey also couldn't tell how long Victor stopped there, if at all, and whether he then proceeded on up to the main building.

Victor was on the hill for less than seven minutes. He turned his lights back on when he was almost at the bottom, after which Corey followed him back to the motel.

Corey then called us to relate what had happened. None of us had any idea what Victor was up to.

Alex Vogel's anxiety was through the roof.

He knew all along that the trial was going to be difficult and an uphill struggle; Andy had been upfront about that. Hike was far more negative, but Alex had learned that Hike was Hike.

Alex had initially been hopeful; it was exciting that they were going to fight back, present their case and try to convince the jury. That hope was gradually waning as reality was setting in; the prosecution's case was just too powerful.

Andy had said that he wanted to speak to Alex that morning before court started to discuss whether he should testify in his own defense. Alex wanted to; he understood that no one else could explain his story or his actions.

But he also knew the potential for disaster. His actions were illogical and stupid at best, incriminating at worst. He knew what a good prosecutor would be able to do to him, and he dreaded destroying his own chances.

So the ten-minute drive in the van to the courthouse that morning, never a fun-filled drive, was even more nerve-racking than usual. As always, the guards said almost nothing. He wanted to talk to them about his predicament, to talk to anyone, but he knew that would be insane.

Instead he would talk to Andy.

When they arrived, the guards unlocked the handcuffs connecting him to the seat and just kept them attached to his two wrists. He had gotten used to that humiliation, but it had taken a while.

He was halfway from the van to the courthouse when the two shots rang out. The first one hit Alex Vogel in the chest and sent him flying. The second would have hit Alex as well, but because he was already on the way down, it went past him and hit a guard in the shoulder.

Alex Vogel was dead before he hit the ground.

Something is going on . . . some kind of commotion.

It seems to be toward the rear of the courthouse, maybe in the judge's chambers, which is back there, or maybe outside. The three bailiffs and the court reporter left and went in that direction. When the court clerk, Rita Gordon, came back about three minutes later, she looked stunned.

"What's going on, Rita?"

"I don't know."

"Come on, Rita."

"They wouldn't let me back there, Andy. I swear I don't know, but everybody is freaked out."

I am worried about this; Alex was supposed to be here by now. He is always brought in through the rear. I hope he didn't do anything stupid like try to escape.

"Andy, come with me, please."

It's Norman Trell, who has seemingly appeared from nowhere. He also looks shaken. Something is very wrong.

"What the hell is going on, Norman?"

He doesn't answer because he's already walking away. I'm supposed to follow him. I don't want to because I know I am not going to like what I hear when we get to wherever we're going. But I've got no choice; I need to know.

We head to Judge Mahomes's chambers. He's sitting behind his desk, not wearing his robe, but instead is in a sport shirt and khakis. It's uncharacteristic of him to not be in his robe when meeting with lawyers.

"Will somebody please tell me what has happened?"

"I'm sorry to have to tell you that Alex Vogel was shot and killed outside the courthouse a short while ago."

I feel like Marcus has punched me in the stomach. "How . . . by a guard?"

Mahomes shakes his head. "No, there was apparently a sniper. There is a great deal of confusion, and I haven't been updated since I was given the news."

This is so shocking and horrible that I can't seem to find a place to put it in my mind. I don't have a mental compartment for it. I've been spending months thinking and strategizing about how to save Alex, and in one awful moment, there is no saving him. There is no jury, no judge, no arguments, no evidence . . . nothing. There is no Alex.

I stand up. "I need to get out of here."

"I think the area might be in lockdown, Andy. You can wait in here."

For some reason it is jarring that the judge just called me Andy. He never does that; I would have guessed he didn't even know my first name. It's not important, yet it's totally important. It's a sign that the world has changed.

I sit back down and not a word is spoken for somewhere between two and thirty minutes; I honestly have no idea. Then the word comes that the lockdown has ended. The judge asks if the perpetrator has been captured, and the answer is a negative shake of the head.

I stand up, leave the chambers, and then the courthouse, I

hope for the last time. Laurie is waiting for me at the top of the steps and she hugs me. A long one.

Neither of us says a word until we are home, and for a while afterward. Laurie pours two glasses of wine, and the first words spoken are when she holds up her glass.

"To Alex."

Within the hour, the house fills with people.

Corey, Marcus, Sam, Willie, even Hike . . . they all come over, although I don't think Laurie called any of them. Everybody seems to need to be with everyone else, except me. I'd rather be alone.

I'm going to beat the shit out of myself with guilt, justified or not, and I'd just as soon start now.

But that is going to have to be delayed since Corey seems intent on turning this into a team meeting. "This was Victor; there's no question about it. When I heard what happened, I went to the motel, and he wasn't there."

"We should have had him covered around the clock," I say.

Corey shakes his head. "We didn't have the manpower."

"We could have hired someone. That's what good lawyers do; they hire people when they need them."

"Andy . . ." Laurie's telling me not to start blaming myself. Good luck with that.

"It's my fault," Sam says. "I should have suggested that we put a GPS device on his car."

"He's smart," Corey says. "He would have found it."

"Not where I would have put it."

Willie says, "We need to nail him."

"Me," Marcus says.

It's the clearest syllable I've ever heard him utter, and the meaning is just as clear. Marcus doesn't want to wait for us to get proof that Victor has done something illegal and set the justice system on him.

Marcus knows that Victor is a murderer, knows where he is staying, and wants to deal with him. One on one. Marcus-style.

"Let's go," Willie says, fully associating himself with Marcus's opinion.

"No," Laurie says. "That is not how we do things."

Hike speaks up for the first time. "It's how Victor does things."

Laurie nods. "I know. But we are better than him."

"There is nothing I would like better than to see him die a painful death," I say. "But it would run contrary to our interests."

Nobody says anything, though I see Corey nod in agreement.

I continue, "We have two responsibilities here. One of them has been our goal all along: we need to prove that Alex was not a murderer. That doesn't change because he's not here anymore. It has become an imperative.

"The other is to stop them from doing what they are doing. This isn't just about Victor. He's got bosses, and this is a wide conspiracy. We cannot let them accomplish whatever it is they have set out to do. That hasn't changed either. We have already lost, but we cannot let them win."

"Are we any closer to figuring it out?" Corey asks.

"I don't know what 'it' is," I say. "But I might know where."

I ask Laurie to hire a couple of outside investigators that we can trust, preferably retired cops, to maintain surveillance on Victor for the hours that we can't. Then I suggest that we reconvene in the morning, after I've had a chance to think this through.

"Sounds like a plan," Laurie says.

People get up to leave, but I ask Willie to wait a second. "We need to talk about Aggie."

"There's nothing to talk about. She's part of our family now. Sondra would never give her up, and I ain't about to either. And Cash? There's no way he is letting her out of his sight. They're buddies."

"Thanks, Willie. I promised Alex that no matter what happened, we'd make sure she was in a great home."

"Then you kept your promise, because she ain't going to have a bad day for the rest of her life."

Alex Vogel was right all along: he was the target. He'd heard Bledsoe accurately on the boat; they were there for him. That's why killing two out of three didn't save Bledsoe and Phillips from their own deaths; they were sent for Vogel, and they missed. They were zero for one. To make matters much worse, they'd probably told Victor that Vogel was dead.

Big Tony also told us that Vogel was the target, but we didn't realize that he meant the sole target. It turns out that Stephen Mellman and Robert Giarrusso were collateral damage; they were in the wrong place at the wrong time.

If that's the case, and I'm positive that it is, then Giarrusso's new drug, the one that the three were going to start a new company to produce, has nothing to do with what is going on. If it did, then Giarrusso would have been in the crosshairs, not Alex.

Giarrusso would have been the one to know all there was to know about that drug; he invented the damn thing. Alex admitted to me that he knew nothing at all about the science, so how could he be a danger to them?

We got thrown by the stolen filing cabinet and that it contained information about Giarrusso's drug. But Robert Giarrusso's house had not been broken into, and much more information about the drug would likely have been found there. That's where he created the damn thing. And how would Victor and his people have even known that Giarrusso's drug information was in Alex's possession?

Giarrusso's drug wasn't why they took the cabinet; it was to get access to whatever else was in there. Alex said it was other work material. I just wish I knew what that material was, if there was anything else, and if any of it is significant. The other thing I wish I knew was whether anything else was taken from that house.

This is about what Alex knew, because whatever knowledge he possessed constituted a threat to Victor and the assholes he is working with and for. It wasn't simply about getting Alex out of the way; the justice system had been doing that quite successfully and was likely to continue to do so.

Alex had no idea what he knew that made him so valuable and vulnerable, but the bad guys were afraid that it could become apparent to him at any time. So they ended that possibility by killing him.

The answer has to have something to do with Pharmacon. That was the only source of big money in Alex Vogel's life. Unless he was withholding information from me, which I suppose is possible, then his life was dominated by his work. Nothing else was important enough or lucrative enough to interest people like Victor.

I call Sam and ask him if he had gotten a list of investors in Pharmacon, as I had requested.

"I have it. I wasn't sure if you still wanted it. You know, because . . ."

"I do. Tell me the highlights."

"I don't know that much about this stuff, but it's got to be unusual. About thirty percent of the shares are owned within the company, mostly by the top executives, but all the employees above a certain level are in the stock-sharing plan. Another five or six percent are owned by individuals outside the company. They are apparently just regular investors, and no one owns a particularly large piece."

"What about the other sixty-five percent?"

"Owned by companies, but that's where it seems strange. They are a bunch of shell companies, apparently set up for the purpose of this and maybe other investments. If they have other functions, I haven't been able to find them.

"But the weirder thing is these shells are owned by other shells; there is just no way to break through and get any actual names of people that might be involved. But some are definitely foreign.

"One thing is for sure: a lot of lawyers and accountants got rich setting this stuff up."

Sam says he will email me a full report, though he's already told me all I need to know. Robby Divine's money-laundering theory just got put back on the front burner.

If that's the answer, then I assume these shell companies will be selling and then repurchasing the stock over and over. I don't know whether that would require the complicity of executives within the company, but I expect on some level either Eric Buckner, the CEO, or Gerald Bennings, the CFO, must be involved.

The company, in the person of one of those individuals, must have arranged who could buy into the original IPO. Robby Divine said that he had no interest in it, but my guess is that he would have been shut out either way. The stock was destined to go to these shell companies.

Some internal executive or executives must be friendly to the laundering scheme. Way too much effort and focus has gone into Pharmacon for it to be just another company; they had to be welcoming of the efforts, if not directing them. Bennings is the most likely candidate; as the CFO, he would have been on the front lines. I don't know that Buckner would have cared who was buying the stock; his concern would have been the price.

But I still come back to the same question: What could Alex Vogel have known that would be so dangerous to their scheme? If he knew about the money laundering, he would have told me. There would have been no reason to withhold it, and it would obviously have been in his best interest to share it with me.

He had to know something else. Could it have been the identities of one or more of the actual investors? Could that person have been so obviously toxic that it could have brought the whole thing down? But wouldn't Alex have realized that?

He knew something, and that knowledge caused his death.

I wish he was here so I could ask him about it.

This is a trip I never expected to make.

Laurie and I are going to the Jefferson Home for Seniors in Rockland County to see about the possibility of my mother moving in there. It's not urgent, since my mother passed away more than a decade ago, but it can't hurt to prepare.

Corey had followed Victor to this place the other night, though Corey has no idea what he did here or why he came. We're heading today to check out the place, pretending to be assessing it as a home for my beloved but already-departed mother.

We're doing it for two reasons. One is that we have nothing else to do, and the other is that if it's interesting to Victor, it's interesting to me.

We have given ourselves a one-week deadline to get somewhere. If we haven't made real progress by that time, then we are going to tell Pete Stanton, the state police, and the FBI everything we know and suspect.

None of that will be enough for them to make an arrest, but it will be more than enough to get them to check Victor out. Once they do, I hope they will find out that he is wanted for other crimes, and they can arrest him. I would say it is a safe bet that Victor has not spent his life on the right side of the law.

My fear, and it gnaws at me constantly, is that Victor will complete whatever he's doing and go back to whatever rock he lives under, probably in another country, and then we will have lost him. That would be a disaster that would haunt me for the rest of my life.

So, no pressure.

The Jefferson Home for Seniors, as Corey accurately described, sits on top of a hill, about a quarter mile up from the main road. That main road is not exactly the FDR Drive either, but at least it's paved. The road that goes up the hill is 100 percent dirt.

We head up toward the home, and when we're about two-thirds of the way there, we pass a small shed. Corey said that he thinks Victor might briefly have stopped at that shed, but he couldn't be sure because of the distance and darkness.

"Stop for a second," Laurie says. "Let's take a look."

I stop and she gets out. She opens the door to the shed, then quickly closes it and gets back in the car. "Just a pumping station."

I don't know what I was hoping for, but a pump wasn't it. We drive farther up the hill and park at the main building. Half a dozen cars are in the parking lot; I would assume they are either staff or people visiting someone who lives here.

A woman answers the door and greets us with a smile. "Hello, can I help you?"

"We're interested in finding a place for my mother to live. She's getting on in years, and we want to make sure—"

She interrupts my lying about my mother's life status. "I understand, but I'm sorry. At the moment we have no availabilities. We never exceed our set limit because we do not want it to impact our services."

Laurie smiles her understanding. "That's fine; Mother probably won't be ready to make the move for months. We just like to be prepared. We've heard such good things about your facility that we thought we should see it."

"Well, I'm certainly happy to show you around. My name is Tina Cheney; I'm the house director. Please call me Tina. Come in."

"That would be wonderful, thank you, Tina," Laurie says, introducing us as Edna and Corey. Laurie appears to be not that original at name creation.

So we start off on the tour. The place seems to be generally busy; staff members are doing things . . . cleaning, baking, and working on what seems to be a makeshift stage in a large meeting room.

"This is our rec room," Tina says. "I'm sorry for all the commotion, but Sunday is our family day. We get a lot of visitors, and the residents put on a little show. They love it."

Four people, all elderly, are playing cards at one of the tables.

"Look, honey," Laurie says. "They're playing bridge." Then, to Tina, "Mother loves bridge. She played in tournaments back in the day." Laurie is pouring it on a little thick.

We check out the rest of the facility, which is quite nice and comfortable. Laurie especially seems to like it; maybe she is planning to dump me here in a couple of years.

When we finish, we sit down for a cup of coffee as Tina has more to tell us and also invites us to ask any questions we might have. "We are a completely self-contained facility. A full kitchen with our own chef, a generator that will always provide heat and water even in adverse weather conditions or if county services should be interrupted for any reason, a nurse on the premises . . ."

"What about security?" I ask. "You're in an isolated location up here. We saw a man while driving up the road who didn't look like he belonged here. He was standing near the shed."

She seems genuinely surprised. "Really? I have no idea who that could be. There is a police station less than half a mile away, so they could be here very quickly, should that ever be necessary. There is also a hospital only a mile away, with a very efficient ambulance service. The residents here feel quite safe, and justifiably so."

We ask a few more questions that we basically have no interest in, and Tina gives us a price list. She tells us to call when Mom is ready, and she hopes there will be availabilities then.

We thank her and leave. When we get to the car, I look down the hill. This would be an easy place to defend; only one way up the hill, and no chance to conceal the approach.

Is that what Victor wants? To use this place like it's the Alamo? Or maybe Victor's mother is here playing bridge, and he came to visit her. That makes as much sense as anything else.

When we get in the car, I say, "Mom played in bridge tournaments back in the day?"

Laurie shrugs. "I was in character; I went with it."

Why the hell don't you put me on retainer? My hourly rate is a million five."

I'm back talking to Robby Divine, this time in his office on Fifty-seventh Street off Madison Avenue in Manhattan. The small two-room office houses just Robby and his assistant. I'm sure it's ample for what he does, which is simply invest in stuff. As he once told me, the only thing his company builds is wealth, and all he needs is a computer and a phone.

Robby always complains when I bug him for information and expertise, but I think down deep he likes it. It gives him the opportunity to simultaneously show off and complain, which I suspect are two of his favorite things. He's wearing his Cubs cap and is actually in a good mood today because they just beat the Mets three straight at Citi Field.

"A million five an hour? I don't have the budget for that. Do you rent out in ten-minute increments?"

He frowns. "I should have known. What do you want to talk about today? Pharmacon again?"

"You got it. I'm still beating my head against the Pharmacon wall. I think you're right that the money is dirty and that they're laundering it."

"When was the last time I was wrong? Oh, I remember now . . . never."

"Sixty-five percent of the stock was bought by shell companies, and the parent companies of the shells are also shells. The ownership is impossible to trace."

He nods. "There you go."

"But why Pharmacon? Would someone in the company be in on it?"

He thinks for a few moments. "Probably. Especially in terms of the IPO and setting up the investors. It sold out, which means they probably turned people away. Somebody had to make that call."

"Who would that be? Gerald Bennings? He's the CFO."

"Definitely; he's a slimy piece of garbage."

"You sent me to him; you told me was the guy to talk to."

Robby shakes his head. "I told you he's smart and knows what he's doing. I never said he was a decent human being."

"But how could they be making big money off of this?"

"I never said they were making big money. I said they were laundering money they already had. That can be just as valuable, depending on the situation."

"But to do that, wouldn't they have to keep buying and selling the stock? Or at least selling?"

He doesn't answer, but instead walks over to his computer and types some information in. Then, "Volume is very low."

"Exactly." I already knew that from Edna's cousin Freddie. "Why would that be? How does that fit with the theory?"

"It doesn't."

"Could they have inside information that the stock is going to go up? What about if they just invented a new drug?" I'm back to thinking that maybe Robert Giarrusso's drug is what this is about.

Robby shakes his head. "No, that's not how this industry works. It takes years to bring a drug to market; there is all kinds of testing in the lab, then on animals, then humans, then you fight with the FDA. If this is mob money, they're not in it for the long haul. They are looking for a quick hit. If you came here looking for a tip to buy a stock, it wouldn't be Pharmacon."

"Would the SEC have a role to play here?"

"Sure, take this to them and your grandkids can wheel you to their offices the day they make their ruling."

I thank Robby for his time and leave. The only thing I got from this meeting is depressed.

I'm driving home during rush hour through the Lincoln Tunnel, which means I would get their faster by walking. Laurie travels distance faster on her exercise bike than these cars are moving.

But it gives me time to think.

Robbie is right. They are not making big money by laundering. All they're doing is washing money that they already have. I'm sure that's valuable, but would they be killing people like this to accomplish that laundering? I don't think so.

They're also spending money like crazy. Russo and his people didn't come cheap. They wouldn't spend that kind of money unless they were going to make an entire trainload of it.

But Robby is also right about something else. They're not in it as simple investors. First of all, you don't have to murder to do that; all you do is call your broker. More important, there is no reason that the stock would be considered a particularly good investment.

Robby doesn't think it is, and he is as wired into these things and as knowledgeable as they come. He said Pharmacon would not be a tip he'd ever give me. Even more significant, none other than Alex Vogel said the same thing. He wouldn't be specific as to why, but he was clear that he, Giarrusso, and Mellman weren't giving up much by leaving the company before it went public. He implied that its prospects were fairly bleak.

So is there something he didn't know?

Or was there something he did?

Pete, I need your help. And you need mine."

In response to an approach like that, Pete Stanton would ordinarily insult me and tell me to get lost. He'd say I was an ambulance chaser and someone willing to defend the lowest of the low to make a fee. I'd tell him he was a clownish cop who might mistakenly handcuff himself.

Typical friend stuff.

He'd eventually help, but not before putting me through conversational torture.

Not this time, and I think there are two reasons for that. One is the tone of my voice; it is deadly serious and as far from friendly banter as a voice could be. The other is that I am standing at the front door of his home at 8:00 A.M. on a Saturday morning.

"Come on in," he says, which is exactly what I would expect a good friend to say.

We go into his kitchen, where he has a pot of coffee already made. He pours me a cup, but before I can say anything, he says, "I don't think Vogel was guilty."

That surprises me, so I ask him why he said it.

"The connection to Phillips and Bledsoe, especially the fact that they chartered the boat that day. Those guys weren't going fishing."

"Vogel was definitely innocent. They killed him, just like they killed Carla D'Antoni, Phillips, Bledsoe, and Big Tony."

"You think you would have gotten him off?"

"I think it was less than fifty-fifty, but I wish I had the chance to find out."

"Why did they need him out of the way?"

"Because he knew something that could destroy everything they built."

"Tell me about it."

So I tell him, first detailing everything I know and how I know it. They I move on to what I believe, but can't prove.

In a few cases I describe things that Alex Vogel told me, which is technically a breach of privilege, even though the client is deceased. Somehow I don't think Alex would mind.

Pete takes it all in, not interrupting or questioning anything. When I'm finished, he asks, "So what do you need?"

"I need to get hold of Judge Mahomes; he has to issue a search warrant. You have the credibility to get that done."

"That may be tough on Saturday. Why Mahomes?"

"Because he's a part of it; it was his courtroom that was violated. He'll want to do it. We don't have much in the way of facts to go on; we're pressing the envelope here. So Mahomes is our best shot, but you'll still have to do some persuading. Rita Gordon knows how to reach him."

Rita is the court clerk and a good friend; I've already called her and she's promised to help.

"Okay," Pete says without hesitation. "I'm all in."

"Thank you. You're also going to have to get the state cops in on it. You won't have jurisdiction."

"That won't be a problem."

"You sure? You think they'll take your word for this?"

He nods. "I'll tell them what you told me. But that's not why they'll be there."

"Then why?"

"Because if we're right, they'll want to be in on it. And if we're wrong, then they've only wasted a couple of hours. It's a no-brainer; they'll be on board."

I stand up. "Then let's do it."

aurie and I leave the house at 5:00 A.M.

We want to be in place in plenty of time, though our presence isn't completely necessary. Marcus and Corey are also in the loop and know their respective responsibilities, and they've been on the job since midnight.

Just in case.

On the way, I say to Laurie, "I need to be there when it happens."

"Andy, we've talked about this. You agreed this is not your strength."

"I know, but now I'm changing my mind. I'm aware that this sounds stupid, but I'm going to be Alex's eyes and ears. It's something I have to do."

She looks like she's about to argue, then says, "Okay, I understand."

"You're the best."

"Yes. I am." She hands me the gun. I'm nervous about even touching it, so she tells me that the safety is on. I'm still nervous about touching it, but I don't tell her that.

At a quarter to seven, Corey calls with a simple message: "He's on the move."

"Good. Don't stay anywhere within his sight line; we know where he is going."

In truth I don't know for sure, but I'm damn near positive and betting a lot on it. Because if Victor is not coming here, then he's going somewhere else, and the results could be catastrophic.

I call Pete and tell him that we are a go. Then Laurie drops me off and I get in position. She drives off and goes to get in place herself.

I'm wearing a jacket even though it is way too warm for it to be necessary. I need a place to keep the handgun, and I'm afraid that if I keep it in my belt, or even in my pants pocket, I might shoot my foot off. Or worse.

I keep my hand in the same pocket, trying to keep the gun from being jostled. It's no doubt ridiculous and unnecessary to do so, but it makes me feel better. I don't go anywhere near the trigger.

We're all set. All we can do is wait and hope we're right.

The pounding on the door started at 6:55.

Gerald Bennings was sleeping when it began, which is why it took him a few minutes to get his bearings and go to the door to see what the hell was going on.

By the time he got there, the door was no longer functioning as intended. That's because it had been knocked down by police uninterested in whether they were disturbing Bennings's sleep.

Pete Stanton led the charge, a courtesy granted by the Paramus police, since that is where Bennings's house is located. Paterson and Paramus cops have conducted a number of joint operations in the past, so Pete had friends there who were willing and anxious to be part of this operation.

Pete handed the warrant to Bennings. Judge Mahomes had signed it eighteen hours earlier. Pete then insisted that Bennings leave the house, graciously allowing him to get dressed first. Once he was out of the house, so was Pete.

He had gone over in detail with the Paramus cops what they should take, and two of Pete's men stayed behind as well. The instructions, while detailed, also contained the directive "If in doubt, take it."

Bennings was vocal in proclaiming his outrage and his

innocence of any possible wrongdoing. He insisted that he be told what they were looking for, but nobody cared about his insistence.

As Pete was leaving, he got a good look at the man.

Gerald Bennings sounded angry, but he looked scared.

I expected Victor would be here at seven thirty, but he beats that by five minutes.

I hear the car pull up; it's a windy day so I don't know if Laurie can hear it from where she is. She doesn't have a straight sight line to it either, but she might see the dust that the car must have raised on the dry dirt road.

The next sound I hear, besides my heart pounding, is the car door opening but not closing. It's a sign that Victor only plans to be here for a few seconds. He doesn't know it, but his plans are about to change.

The shed door opens, and the first thing Victor sees is me, Andy Carpenter, leaning against the water tank and holding a gun on him. I've had guns held on me before, but I've never been the one doing the holding. It's significantly better this way, but I'm still nervous as hell.

I take comfort in that the worst than can happen is that the gun will accidentally go off and Victor will get shot. I could live with that, even if Victor couldn't.

Victor looks surprised when he sees me, but not panicked. Far from it. This guy always thinks he is in control, and until now he's always been right.

"Where the hell have you been?" I ask, trying to keep the

nervousness out of my voice. "We've been worried sick about you."

He doesn't say anything, so I add, "This is the time you raise your hands."

He pauses a moment, conveying the impression that whether he raises his hands is his decision, not mine. When he does raise them, he hits the top of the shed. It makes me realize how big this guy is.

Victor is probably six-four and must weigh two-fifty. He could have been a tight end for the Giants, if he hadn't chosen to be a scumbag killer. Bad career choice.

"You will not leave here alive." He points up and to the left, which is in the direction of the main house. "They will die, but you will die faster and easier. Consider yourself lucky."

"On the other hand, I could shoot you now, which would be a net plus for humanity." If my hand wasn't shaking so much, I think there would be more chance he would be intimidated.

Before Victor can respond, he is pushed from behind up against the wall. A hand comes around and deftly removes his gun from his pocket. The other hand takes something out of the other pocket. Victor reacts more to that, so I know what it must be.

"Victor, have you met Marcus Clark?"

Victor doesn't answer, so I say, "Step outside."

He exits the shed along with Marcus, and I follow them, still nervously holding the gun. I know that the correct thing is to just stand there like this until the police arrive, but I made a promise to Marcus.

I make it a habit never to break a promise to Marcus.

Marcus is standing between Victor and his running car, and I say, "If you can get to your car, you're free to go."

It's a complete lie; the police are blocking off the road below and Laurie is up at the Jefferson Home. But if I was okay with the possibility of shooting Victor, I'm certainly fine with lying to him.

The cops are not here already because of the deal I made with them to let them be a part of the operation. I was afraid that Victor might detect their presence and be scared off. That was one reason; the other was that promise to Marcus.

For some reason it's somewhat disconcerting to me to realize that Victor seems unfazed by what is happening, as if he can handle things quite well.

He looks at Marcus, who himself looks so unconcerned that I think he might actually be asleep. I expect Victor to make a move, and he does, just not the one I expected.

He whirls and knocks the gun out of my hand. A wave of panic hits me as we both go for the gun and I realize that he is going to beat me to it. And he does beat me, but he still comes in second, with me a distant third. Marcus gets there first.

Marcus kicks the gun and it goes rattling down the hill. At first I think Victor is going to run after it, but Marcus is in the way. Victor makes the smart choice; he goes for the car.

Marcus reaches him before Victor gets to the open car door and knocks him into the side of the car. He could have just shot him instead, since he has Victor's gun in his pocket. But that is not Marcus's style.

Victor bounces off the car and whirls around, his face contorted with fury. It's the first emotion I've seen him display.

If someone is going to fight Marcus, and I would strongly recommend against it, anger doesn't help. If you don't want to bring a knife to a gunfight, you don't want to bring rage to a Marcus fight. It makes clear thinking difficult, and if you're going up against Marcus, you've already got enough problems.

Victor rears back and throws a roundhouse right at Marcus's head. It appears to be so powerful that it could knock down a medium-size sequoia. Marcus steps inside it and delivers a straight left into Victor's chest. The thud can likely be heard on Long Beach Island.

Then Marcus follows it with a right to Victor's temple, which sends the piece of garbage staggering backward.

I can't follow it all too well because I am backing down the hill about thirty feet to retrieve my gun, just in case. Based on my previous performance with that gun, we'd probably be better off with it lying on the road.

But I do get to see Marcus completely dismantle Victor. He winds up sitting against the wall of the shed, his head backed against it, close to unconscious, as Marcus prepares to throw a punch that a rhinoceros could not survive.

"Marcus, no!" I don't yell because I care what happens to Victor; I'd be fine to see his brain splattered against the side of the shed. I yell because Pete and the state cops are coming up the hill, and Laurie and one of Pete's cops are coming down from the main building.

What Marcus is about to do, in the eyes of somebody who gives a shit more than I do, could be considered murder at worst and manslaughter at best. So I don't want Marcus to do it because I don't want him to get in legal trouble.

And because I sure as hell don't want another client.

Marcus listens and doesn't throw the punch. I put the gun on the ground because I won't know any of the arriving state cops and I don't want them making a mistake.

Pete and the cops get there and take over. Laurie gives me a hug and I'm embarrassed because my hands are shaking. "You okay?" she asks.

"Yes." Then, "You should know that I didn't cover myself

with glory." I don't tell her what I mean; there will be time for that later.

Marcus comes over to me and hands me what he took out of Victor's left pocket, which is a small vial, sealed at the top.

It is what all this was about.

As search warrants go, this was a classic.

Bennings was careless and obviously never thought anyone would invade his home like that. Plenty of incriminating evidence not only clearly established his guilt, but also the conspiracy.

The most damaging documents were two sets of test results for the Pharmacon drug Loraxil. One included the results of the real-world testing, which showed a drug of limited effectiveness against the superbugs it was supposed to destroy. It also showed significant and unintended side effects, which were problematic at best and disqualifying at worst. Those documents were duplicates of the ones that were in Alex Vogel's stolen filing cabinet.

The other set of documents portrayed a much rosier picture, and in those Loraxil came off as a drug that was not only promising, but likely a breakthrough. Those were the documents submitted to the FDA, which would have had them leaning toward approval.

But ultimate approval wasn't enough for Bennings and his investors; they wanted it to happen immediately. And even that would not satisfy them; they wanted it approved in such a way as to send the stock soaring.

Evidence showed that a husband and wife named Radford in New York State came down with a superbug infection, and that Loraxil cured it. That was impressive to the FDA, but not conclusive. More pressure was needed, as was a stunning event to pressure the FDA to act.

So the deadly bacteria was going to be put into the water supply at the Jefferson Home for Seniors. Water came up the hill from the county, then pumps in the shed sent it the rest of the way up to the main house.

Two tanks held the water. The situation was perfect for Victor; he could easily infect the water, and the unknowing people at the home would drink it. It would be contained to the people staying at the house, plus the family day visitors.

Two things would then happen. First, the FDA would find that Pharmacon, having never gotten approval, did not have the supplies to treat the contained epidemic. People would die, possibly by the dozens.

Second, the public would go nuts and panic in their fear that the superbug was going to end the world, with only Loraxil and Pharmacon able to stop it.

The stock would react accordingly. Estimates were that the $10 stock would top out at $150, which would mean the initial $600 million valuation would become $9 billion.

You can buy a lot of Joseph Russos with $9 billion.

Usually our victory parties are held at Charlie's.

This time is different because we wanted Aggie, Cash, Sebastian, Simon Garfunkel, and Tara to attend. That seemed a little much for a sports bar typically patronized by humans.

So in addition to those five dogs, as well as the twenty-five we have up for adoption, Laurie, Corey, Hike, Edna, Willie, Sondra, and Marcus are here. Pete and Vince have come as well, since I told them we'd be bringing food and beer in from Charlie's. Beth Morris and her husband have stopped by, and I am happy to report that Ricky is here as well, having come home from camp yesterday. He wouldn't miss an event with this many dogs for the world.

The mood is far more subdued than at previous victory parties, for obvious reasons. But I think we all understand that we accomplished a great deal: we saved lives.

Corey and I haven't had a chance to talk for a while, so he has a bunch of questions he'd like answered. The first one is "Why did they have to kill Alex?"

"Because he knew the real test results, the ones they did not submit to the FDA. He wasn't supposed to have seen them, but once he did, he had to go. They also were in that filing cabinet. Alex didn't realize that what he knew was significant because he had no way of knowing they were committing fraud by lying to the FDA."

"If he didn't realize that what he knew was significant, why was it so important that they kill him?"

"Because approval of this drug, in light of the public's panic about the superbug, would become big news. He was the only one outside the conspiracy that knew the truth: that the drug was not an effective one. If he revealed that, it would destroy their chance to make a fortune."

"How did you figure it out?"

"I wasn't really sure I had until Victor showed up at that shed. But for one thing, the stock going up was the only possible way for them to make huge money. And Carla D'Antoni had told her sister that she was going to be giving her a stock tip."

"They told her about the stock? Why would they do that?"

"You didn't hear?" I ask. "The state police arrested Eric Buckner this morning. Bennings turned on him; he's claiming that Buckner gave all the orders and he was just following them."

Corey nods. "The ultimate loyal employee."

"Right. But Bennings drew them a picture of the whole operation. Buckner had been dating Carla; she referred to him to her sister as Rick. But that's who she meant. They think he gave her all the cash, but he was apparently okay with her being killed once she was no longer useful to them. And she must have overheard talk about the stock."

"How was she useful?"

"By telling them where Alex kept his work papers, and when he would be on the boat. Also, another tip-off was when Big Tony was killed. The day before, I had asked Bennings if he had heard of Victor. They must have figured out that Big Tony gave us the name; there's no one else it could have been."

Pete comes over to provide a new piece of information. "You

know that couple that got cured? The Radfords? Turned out they didn't have that superbug thing at all; the lab guy was in on it. He tested contaminated blood, but it wasn't from the Radfords; it was from some poor guy in Omaha that they infected with it."

"So the Loraxil cured what they had?"

"Any antibiotic would have cured what they had."

"What about Victor?" I ask.

"He was Russian Mafia. Interpol has three warrants out on him, so when he gets out of the hospital, he'll be going away for a long time."

Then Pete delivers what in friendship land is the ultimate compliment: "I gotta admit, you didn't screw this up."

Laurie comes over and points out into the middle of the dog-play area, where Aggie is wrestling with Simon Garfunkel and Tara. That fantastic black Lab, Bruiser, has already gone to a great home, which is what this is all about.

"You think Aggie remembers and misses Alex?" I ask.

"I don't know," Laurie says. "But she is happy, and safe, and loved, and that is the best we can do. And you know what? That's pretty good."